THE SECRET
AT THE GATEHOUSE

Books by

CAROLYN KEENE

Nancy Drew Mystery Stories

Dana Girls Mystery Stories

"Wait a minute," McCarter advised. "We
might be walking into a trap."

The Secret at the Gatehouse

THE SECRET AT THE GATEHOUSE

By

CAROLYN KEENE

Grosset & Dunlap, *Publishers*
NEW YORK

CONTENTS

CONTENTS

CHAPTER I

A MYSTERIOUS MESSAGE

"Whose idea was it to take this short cut through these dark woods?" inquired Evelyn Starr of her companions, Jean and Louise Dana. The three friends, students at Starhurst School for Girls, had attended the autumn pet show at the Cedar Crest Kennels. Now they were returning to the dormitory some distance away.

"I guess it was mine," confessed Jean Dana, pausing to pluck cockleburs from her silk stockings. "At any rate it is the shortest way back."

"We've seen new and interesting country, anyway," added Louise Dana. She was the older of the two sisters, dark, and inclined to be serious.

"Oh, I'm not complaining," laughed Evelyn good-naturedly. "It's just that I always get a shivery feeling whenever I'm in the woods. Right now I can believe very easily that someone is following us."

1

"That's strange," acknowledged Jean. "You know, I've had the same sensation but I hated to mention it lest I sound silly."

"Listen!" commanded Louise suddenly.

The three girls paused. Distinctly they could hear back of them the crackling of dry leaves among the trees.

"Someone *is* following us," Jean whispered in alarm. "Let's find out who it is."

Before the girls could make a move to investigate, a black and white hunting dog padded from the forest into the tiny clearing. Going over to Louise, he stood still and waited to be patted.

"Hello, doggie," she laughed as she bent down to examine his collar. "You gave us a real fright for a minute! Have you lost your master?"

"He looks like one of those valuable hunting dogs that won a blue ribbon at the pet show!" exclaimed Jean. "Do you suppose he ran away from the kennel?"

"We're a mile from there now," declared Evelyn. "It scarcely seems likely. But wherever he came from he seems to be a valuable dog."

"I suppose we should take him back to the kennel and inquire," Louise ventured doubtfully.

"And get a demerit for reaching the dormitory late?" Jean asked, shaking her head. "You know that never would do. We ought to hurry along, so we shan't be late."

"We have at least two miles yet to cover," Evelyn added, giving weight to Jean's argument. "The dog should go back to the kennels by himself."

"He should," agreed Louise dryly, "but he probably will not. He acts as if he'd like to belong to us."

As the girls started to walk on, the hunting dog solemnly followed, not once varying his steady pace. In vain they scolded the animal, telling him to "go home."

"What shall we do if he follows us all the way to Starhurst?" Evelyn asked in dismay. "Keep him and try to locate his owner?"

"That's all we can do," agreed Louise.

The girls trudged on, pulling their sweaters closer about them, for it had grown chilly. Glancing back a few minutes later, as they reached the main road, they were dismayed to see that the dog still trailed them, trotting along patiently.

"I wish he would see a rabbit and chase it," Louise remarked with a sigh.

Almost as she spoke, the dog stiffened to an attitude of attention. With a loud bark he suddenly rushed down the road past the astonished girls. He headed straight toward an old lady seated on a low stone wall which bordered a field.

"Oh, gracious!" exclaimed Evelyn in horror. "He means to attack her!"

With one accord the three girls raced toward the fence but need not have feared for the old lady's safety. The dog, instead of attacking the woman began to lick her hand.

"Why, he must belong to her!" exclaimed Jean in relief.

As the chums drew closer they could not fail to observe that the old lady had been crying. Seeing them, she hastily brushed away her tears and tried to smile.

"Good afternoon," said Louise pleasantly. "Is this your dog?"

The sad woman shook her head. "No, the dog is not mine, but I know him. He was raised at the Warrington estate from a very fine litter."

"Warrington Manor is not far from here, is it?" remarked Jean.

Everyone knew the famous place, where generations of the important old family had lived.

"This stone wall bounds a portion of the land. Yonder through the trees you can see the back of the mansion. On the other road," the old lady's voice broke as she pointed, "is the little gatehouse. I—I lived there going on forty-five years."

Louise gazed first at the roof of the big house barely visible through the trees, then at the frail little person beside her.

"Don't you live there now?" she inquired gently.

Tears began to roll down the distressed woman's cheeks again. This time she did not try to brush them away.

"Not any more," she answered after a moment. "My husband died a month ago, and a better man there never lived. Mr. Warrington said himself he couldn't ask for a more faithful employee."

"Your husband was the gatekeeper?" inquired Jean thoughtfully.

"Yes, we lived in the little gatehouse on the edge of the estate. I had it fixed up real pretty and cozy like. We stayed there so many years I never thought of the place not belonging to us. I had to leave after my husband died."

"I should think Mr. Warrington would have allowed you to stay," declared Evelyn Starr indignantly.

"Oh, Mr. Warrington didn't realize how much living on the estate meant to me," the woman said sadly. "He says now I must have a better house and not try to work again. I'll be seventy-five my next birthday, coming in March."

"It doesn't seem right to send you away," said Jean, glancing at Louise. Her expression made it plain to her sister that she wished she might help to make this woman happy again.

"A man named Bert Badger is the new watchman," went on the old lady. "He's a good man they tell me, but it doesn't seem right, him being in my husband's place."

"I can understand how you feel," declared

Louise sympathetically. "May we inquire your name?"

"Mrs. Zerbe," the old lady replied. "Mrs. Henry Zerbe. I thought everybody around here knew me."

"We come from Starhurst School for Girls," Louise explained. "This is the first time we have ever been on this road."

"Pretty out here, isn't it?"

"Indeed it is," returned Louise. "I imagine the Warrington estate must be very beautiful."

"It is a wonderful place," Mrs. Zerbe returned, awe in her voice. "And the house is just like a big hotel. Sixty rooms, two elevators, one for the help and one for the folks. There's even a swimming pool!"

"I suppose it is quite a show place," remarked Jean. "Furnished with antiques?"

"Oh, no," the old lady replied quickly, assuming that old furniture was inferior to new. "Everything is just as fine as money can buy. Oriental rugs and bric-a-brac from all parts of the world. Mr. Warrington was a great traveler in his younger day—a good, generous man."

"It doesn't seem very generous of him to put you off the estate," Evelyn commented in a pointed way.

"Oh, Mr. Warrington tried to do the right thing. He gives me a nice pension every month. I get along well enough, only I'm very lonesome for the old gatehouse. Henry and I spent so many happy days there.''

"It must be hard to lose one's home," Louise murmured. "But it's nice that Mr. Warrington is taking care of you."

"Yes, I'm grateful to him," sighed Mrs. Zerbe. "It seems my days are dull, though. Now at the estate, something interesting was always happening. Important folks were coming or going, and usually they would have a pleasant word for Henry and me."

"I suppose you met a number of celebrities, as gatekeepers at such a large place," remarked Jean, hoping the old lady would tell more of her experiences.

"Oh, yes, Mr. Warrington was a great man for entertaining. I've met movie stars, senators, governors, and once a President spent a night at the Manor. I'll never forget my experiences as long as I live. All in all, I'm grateful because I carry wonderful memories of my days there."

Talking of the past seemed to cheer the old lady, and for that reason the girls encouraged her to reveal more. Getting painfully down from the stone wall, she walked along the road with them, the dog following behind.

"The estate isn't as nice as it was years ago," she confided. "Mr. Warrington hasn't the money to spend he once did. It's said his financial affairs are in a muddle."

"It must cost a great deal to keep up such a vast acreage," commented Louise, her gaze roving over the hills.

"Oh, it does! The payroll alone amounts to a small fortune and the taxes are frightful. I heard too that the government has been making trouble for Mr. Warrington."

"What seems to be wrong?" questioned Jean in surprise.

"It's something to do with his business. I never did hear the details."

Before the girls could make further inquiry, a boy on a bicycle came pedaling down the road. The hunting dog began to bark. The lad, leaping off beside the group, glanced directly at the old lady.

"You're Mrs. Zerbe, aren't you?" he inquired.

"That's my name."

"I was on my way to deliver a message to you," the boy told her. "This will save a trip. Here it is."

He handed the woman an envelope bearing a crest. Then, jumping on his bike again, he rode rapidly back the way he had come.

"This looks as if it might be from Mr. Warrington!" Mrs. Zerbe declared excitedly. "Wouldn't it be nice if he should ask me to come back and live on the estate!"

"Why don't you open it and see?" laughed

Evelyn. "Then your suspense will be at an end."

"I can't read without my spectacles and I left them at home. Will one of you girls be so kind as to tell me what it says?"

"Why, of course," said Jean instantly.

She accepted the envelope. Slitting it with a thumb nail, she scanned the message at a glance. Her eyes, raised to meet those of Louise and Evelyn, warned them that the news was not what Mrs. Zerbe had expected.

"Does it say I'm to go back?" the old lady inquired impatiently as Jean hesitated.

"I am afraid not. This is what Mr. Warrington has written:

" 'My dear Mrs. Zerbe:
Will you please telephone to me at the first opportunity as I should like to discuss with you a very important matter. I consider it advisable for you to go to another community until certain investigations are closed. You readily will understand that it never would do to have the secret at the gatehouse made public at this time.' "

"The secret at the gatehouse," Mrs. Zerbe repeated in great agitation. "I shouldn't have allowed you to see the letter! Oh, dear, oh, dear, now what have I done?"

CHAPTER II

VICIOUS DOGS

"DON'T be alarmed, Mrs. Zerbe," Louise said kindly. "You may be sure we'll never repeat the contents of this note, nor anything else you have told us."

"Indeed not," added Jean. "We'll keep the secret to ourselves."

"I shouldn't have talked the way I did," the old lady murmured as the group walked on, the dog following them. "But I do believe I can trust you. Now I must telephone to Mr. Warrington at once!"

By this time the four had reached the outskirts of Penfield. Mrs. Zerbe declared that she would go to the drugstore and call her former employer from there. While the girls were curious to learn more about the mysterious affair connected with the gatehouse, they were too polite to make an outright inquiry. The stranger herself volunteered no additional information.

"Good-bye," she said a few minutes later. "I hope we shall meet again some time—if I don't go away."

The three girls paid no attention to the hunt.

10

ing dog, assuming that the animal would remain with Mrs. Zerbe. As they walked toward Starhurst School, Evelyn glanced back once or twice but did not see the pet. She was relieved.

"I guess we're rid of him at last," she said with a laugh. "My, what an interesting day we've had!"

"I wish we had learned more about that so-called secret at the gatehouse!" Jean remarked thoughtfully. "Sounds mysterious, doesn't it?"

"Yes," agreed her sister soberly, "but I'm more concerned about another matter. Do you realize who Mr. Warrington is, Jean?"

"A wealthy man."

"Obviously. Well, since your memory is so bad, I'll tell you. Richard Warrington is one of the owners of the steamship company which controls the *Balaska!*"

"Uncle Ned's ship!" exclaimed Jean.

"If an investigation is under way, it's easy to guess what might happen. For all we know, Mr. Warrington's difficulties with the government may involve us in a roundabout way. If the steamship company should have to be sold, what would happen to Uncle Ned?"

Jean, startled, stared at her sister in blank astonishment.

"My, but you can think up worries faster than anyone I ever knew!"

"It's all quite possible, isn't it?"

"Yes, I suppose so," Jean admitted reluctantly. "But Uncle Ned never has hinted to us that anything is wrong."

"He may not suspect it. Anyway, he hasn't been home for over a month so we wouldn't know."

"That's true," Jean replied, frowning.

For many years the two girls, who were orphans, had lived with their uncle, Ned Dana, captain of the steamship *Balaska,* and his kindly maiden sister, their Aunt Harriet, at Oak Falls. The household was an unusually happy one, enlivened by the clumsy mishaps of Cora Appel, nicknamed by Jean, Applecore, a loyal but slow-witted maid.

For several seasons Jean and Louise had attended the well-known Starhurst School for Girls, located near Penfield, and supervised by Professor and Mrs. Crandall. There they had won many friends, including Evelyn Starr. However, they had made enemies of Lettie Briggs and Ina Mason, two girls who were regarded as troublemakers and fault finders.

The Dana sisters had delved into their first absorbing mystery while at Starhurst, a story which came to be known as the case, *By the Light of the Study Lamp.* Recently they had enjoyed an adventure on a western ranch, there matching wits with members of a disreputable organization which had absconded with priceless Crown Jewels. The amazing manner in which the Dana girls saved the treasure was started by *The Clue in the Cobweb*.

"I wish we knew more about Mr. Warrington's affairs and how this investigation may affect the steamship line," Louise went on, resuming the discussion. "I can't help being worried."

"Oh, I don't see how Uncle Ned can lose out, regardless of what happens," Jean answered carelessly. "He's such a good captain that if he ever should be without a ship, a dozen companies would want his services."

Louise did not reply, so deep in thought was she. The three girls walked hurriedly to the dormitory, where the Danas took leave of Evelyn. They went directly to their own suite, changed from their hiking clothes, then began to study. Presently there came a light tap on the door.

"Come in," Louise called absently, not getting up.

The door swung back and a tall, dignified woman appeared. Instantly the girl sprang to her feet, upsetting the chair in her confusion.

"Oh, how do you do, Mrs. Crandall," she murmured. "Please forgive me for not opening the door. We thought you were one of the girls."

"I am sorry to disturb you during study

hour," the headmistress said somewhat stiffly. "However, it is necessary. Something will have to be done at once about your dog."

"Our dog!" Jean exclaimed. "Why, we haven't any dog, Mrs. Crandall."

"A hound has been running around the lower corridors. Lettie Briggs gave me to understand she saw the animal with you girls this afternoon."

"Oh," murmured Louise in a faint voice. "It must be the hunting dog that followed us from the pet show."

"If you were the person who brought the animal here I must ask you to get rid of it at once."

"We didn't know the dog followed us after we got to the center of Penfield," Jean explained hurriedly. "He left us in town. We were told he's a valuable pet which came originally from the Warrington estate."

"He trailed us all the way from the Cedar Crest Kennels," Louise added. "I don't know how we'll get him back there."

"Well, that throws a different light on the situation," Mrs. Crandall said in a less severe tone. "I shall have the watchman lock the animal in the tool house for the night. Tomorrow you may go with Mr. Crandall by motorcar to return the dog to its owner."

"Thank you, Mrs. Crandall," murmured Louise. "We will do so."

"I am relieved," replied the headmistress, "that you did not break the rule which forbids pets to be brought into the dormitory. But then, I know you are trustworthy."

When the door had closed behind the woman, Louise and Jean regarded each other grimly.

"So Lettie told her!" Jean muttered. "The little tattletale!"

"How do you suppose she learned that the dog had followed us?" asked Louise in perplexity.

"She must have been trailing us herself! I didn't see her anywhere."

"More than likely she kept out of sight on purpose," Louise declared. "You know Lettie's sneaking ways."

"Don't I! Louise, do you suppose she saw us talking with Mrs. Zerbe?"

"She probably did. Not much ever escapes Lettie's sharp eyes. I only hope she didn't overhear our conversation."

"Especially the part about the mystery at the gatehouse," Jean added with a groan. "All we can do now is to wait and see. Lettie soon will begin to boast about what she knows."

At dinner that evening the Briggs girl made several thinly veiled hints that she knew where the Dana sisters had been during the day. However, she made no reference to Mrs. Zerbe nor to the gatehouse. "I'm relieved so far," sighed Louise later to her sister.

Early the next morning in company with Professor Crandall, the Danas motored to the Cedar Crest Kennels and received profuse thanks from the owners for returning the missing dog. Back at the dormitory once more, the girls were kept busy throughout the day with classes and various sports. As they were preparing for bed after the lights out bell had sounded that night, Jean remarked to her sister:

"Louise, did you notice how Ina Mason and Lettie Briggs were whispering together at the dinner table this evening?"

"Yes, I did," returned Louise. "And they kept glancing at us as if they were planning some scheme! I'll bet they're up to something."

"We'll have to be on guard. They're up to tricks all right. And I can't help but feel their plan may have something to do with our meeting Mrs. Zerbe. I'm beginning to think Lettie has learned something."

Jumping into their separate beds, the sisters soon were fast asleep. Jean had not slept long when suddenly she was aroused by a sound in the hallway. Sitting up in bed, she listened intently.

"Louise!" she called, reaching over and shaking her sister. "What is that noise?"

"What?" she inquired drowsily. "Why, it sounds like an army parading up and down the hall."

Jean leaped from her bed and opened the door, then uttered a faint cry of horror. Louise, hurrying to her sister's side, was astonished to see three huge dogs running up and down the long corridor.

"Well, of all things!" she exclaimed. "Where did they come from?"

"Can't you guess?" Jean asked dryly.

"Lettie Briggs."

"Of course! This was the little trick she thought up to get us into trouble with the headmistress. We'll have to chase these dogs out of here before Mrs. Crandall hears the commotion."

Quickly donning robes and slippers, the Dana girls guided the three hounds down the stairway leading to the lower floor. In passing Lettie's room they heard a sound suspiciously like a giggle.

"Ina and Lettie probably are getting a huge laugh out of this," Jean muttered under her breath. "I'd like to report the matter to Mrs. Crandall."

"We haven't any proof that Lettie is responsible," replied Louise. "The thing to do is to get these animals out of here and say nothing."

The dogs had no collars by which they could be led, and they showed a perverse inclination to go in any but the right direction. To Jean's dismay one of them suddenly made a rush toward Mrs. Crandall's bedroom door, banging against the panel with its full weight.

"Now we're in for trouble," the girl groaned.

In just a moment the door swung open. The headmistress peered into the dark hall.

"Who is there?" she called sharply. "What is the meaning of this commotion?"

Jean and Louise had no opportunity to explain. As they were groping for words, one of the dogs gave a low, savage growl. Before anyone could stave off the attack, the vicious animal leaped upon Mrs. Crandall, seizing one of the woman's arms between its strong jaws.

CHAPTER III

LETTIE'S PRANK

MRS. CRANDALL screamed, and tried to fight off the dog. With no thought that they too might be injured, Jean and Louise rushed to the headmistress's aid, kicking at the beast until it released its hold on her and scurried down the corridor.

"Are you hurt, Mrs. Crandall?" Jean asked anxiously, groping for the electric switch.

When light flooded the hallway, the woman was revealed leaning limply against the wall, her arm bruised and bleeding.

"Oh, Mrs. Crandall," Jean murmured in horror, "you've been bitten. I'll call the doctor at once."

"I am quite able to go to the infirmary by myself," replied the headmistress in a cool voice. "Please put those animals out of the building this minute!"

"Yes, Mrs. Crandall," Louise said contritely. "We're terribly sorry——"

"I'll discuss this with you later," replied the woman. "Please go directly to your rooms as soon as you have driven the dogs out of the dormitory."

Frightened at what had occurred, Jean and Louise lost no time in herding the three hounds into the yard. As the commotion had awakened a number of persons in the dormitory, lights were snapped on in the various wings. Girls began to run into the halls to inquire what was wrong.

"Mrs. Crandall has been bitten by a dog," Louise explained reluctantly. "It is a deep wound, too, and I'm afraid she'll have to have treatments for rabies."

"How dreadful," murmured Evelyn Starr. "It wasn't that dog which followed us from the Cedar Crest Kennels?"

"No," Jean answered briefly. "Someone played a prank to cause trouble for us. I think I can guess who is the person responsible for it too!"

Obeying Mrs. Crandall's order, the Dana girls returned to their suite, refusing to commit themselves further as to the details of the unfortunate affair. Scarcely had they closed their door, when there came a warning tap and Lettie Briggs slipped inside.

"Is Mrs. Crandall badly hurt?" she inquired in a whisper.

"A dog bite always is serious," returned Jean sternly. "I should think you would be ashamed of yourself!"

"Ashamed?" Lettie countered innocently. "Of what? I hope you don't believe I had any-

thing to do with those dogs being in the building!"

"Oh, no!" Louise said in an ironical tone.
"Of course not."

"You better not try to blame me for it,"
Lettie warned the Danas.

Seeing how hopeless the situation was, Jean
and Louise jumped into bed and turned out the
light. In the morning they were relieved to
learn that Mrs. Crandall appeared little the
worse for her misadventure. However, she
carried her arm in a sling and it was known
that she had been given a treatment for rabies.

At assembly exercises the headmistress failed
to appear, but Professor Crandall delivered a
long talk which obviously was directed at Jean
and Louise. At the end of the speech on correct
deportment he sternly requested them to appear
at his office at ten-thirty that morning.

"You're going to catch it!" giggled Lettie,
who chanced to overhear him. "Oh, I do feel
sorry for you girls. Wouldn't it be dreadful if
you were to be expelled?"

The Danas said nothing. They waited until
the girl had gone down the hall to attend French
class, then Jean inquired softly:

"I seem to remember that Ina takes French
at this hour too, doesn't she?"

Louise nodded at the inference. "I was thinking the same thing. Do we dare go to their
rooms now and start a search for clues?"

"Why not?" asked Jean. "We've nothing to lose and everything to gain by trying it. Come on!"

Without attracting any attention, the sisters slipped upstairs and entered the suite occupied by Ina Mason and Lettie Briggs.

"My, what has happened here?" Jean exclaimed as she gazed about her.

Clothes were scattered helter-skelter over the floor. The beds were unmade. Crumbs and bits of other food littered the study tables. Suddenly Jean seized upon an object which had been tossed into the wastebasket.

"An empty can of dog food!" she cried. "What does this mean, Louise?"

"That Lettie and Ina used the food to lure those hounds into the building! Then, they scattered it along the hallways!"

Louise opened the door of the wardrobe closet and peered inside. Though the floor was strewn with old shoes, she noticed in a corner a pile of crumpled newspapers. Lifting them up, she gave a jubilant cry.

"I've found a real clue, Jean! Just look at this!"

The blond girl quickly crossed to the closet where Louise was holding up a dog collar. On the leather, printed in brass studs, appeared the name Sally.

"And here are two others!" the girl added triumphantly, stooping over.

One bore the name Hector, the other that of Captain.

"This is positive proof that Ina and Lettie lured those dogs into the building!" Jean exclaimed. "They hid the collars here, thinking no one ever would come in and find them."

"What I should like to know is, where did they get the dogs in the first place?"

"That's an angle that might bear further investigation," Jean said grimly. "Well, let's get away from here before someone comes and finds us. The time for this class period is nearly up!"

Quickly she wrapped the collars in one of the discarded newspapers and put it under her arm. Then the girls hastened away. As they walked down the deserted hall, discussing the matter somewhat excitedly, they let their voices rise higher than either of them realized. So absorbed were they in what they were saying, that they failed to see Mrs. Crandall standing in the doorway of the infirmary. The headmistress overheard every word of their conversation although they were not aware of the fact.

Returning to their suite, the Dana girls examined the evidence against Lettie and Ina. After further discussion they decided to confront their two tormentors with their discovery.

As Jean started to wrap the collars in their original covering, she suddenly exclaimed over a news story which had caught her eye. It was printed on the front page of the three-day-old paper.

"Louise," she said. "Read this!"

"What is it about, Jean?"

"Mr. Richard Warrington. It says here he is under investigation because of a land deal in connection with the municipal airport!"

Going quickly to her sister's side, Louise read the story over the other's shoulder. The news account was long, offering several angles of the case.

"I wonder how many of these accusations will turn out to be correct," said Louise.

"Mr. Warrington and his family have held such influential positions it doesn't seem as if the things that are being held against him could be true," prophesied Jean.

"I'd like to meet him, wouldn't you?" asked Jean.

"I certainly would," replied her sister. "And I'd like to meet his beautiful daughter Evangeline, too."

"I read somewhere that she is as lovely as her name," said Jean. "Money has not spoiled her at all."

"One of the fashion magazines says she is the best dressed young woman in the country," laughed the older girl.

"Even so, I don't envy her at the moment," said her sister. "What good are beauty, money and handsome clothes if one's father is under investigation?''

"I've heard Aunt Harriet say,'' Louise reminded the younger Dana, "that a wealthy person often is the victim of circumstances because of his money.''

"That's true,'' agreed Jean. "It may be found that Mr. Warrington trusted someone who has turned against him.''

"Perhaps,'' added Louise. "But there's one thing that bothers me. Don't forget. There's some secret at the gatehouse in connection with his affairs!''

During the conversation Jean had been cutting the article from the newspaper. Now she folded it and placed it in her handkerchief box for future reference.

"It's ten-twenty-five,'' Louise stated a moment later, "and time to face Professor Crandall. Shall we tell him the truth about Lettie and the dogs? I hate to tattle on anyone.''

"So do I, but I don't like to be suspected of something I haven't done!''

As it developed, there was no need for the Dana girls to tell a thing. As they entered his private office, Professor Crandall greeted them cordially.

"I wish to express my appreciation to you for the courageous way in which you tried to protect Mrs. Crandall from that vicious dog last evening,'' he said cheerfully.

Jean and Louise exchanged quick, puzzled glances.

"I might say that I am making a complete investigation of the whole affair. Since I spoke at assembly this morning I have acquired interesting information absolving you girls and implicating Ina Mason and Lettie Briggs."

Professor Crandall talked on. Jean and Louise were so surprised at the turn of events that they scarcely heard a word he said. Once outside the office they breathed sighs of relief.

"Well, did you ever!" exclaimed Jean. "How do you suppose he learned the truth?"

"I have no idea. Lettie and Ina will be fortunate if they're not expelled."

During the day the Dana sisters did not see the two culprits, and it was rumored that Lettie and Ina had been sent to their rooms after a lengthy session with Professor Crandall. Although the man usually was calm, he had been aroused by the attack on his wife.

Louise and Jean did not reveal their own knowledge of the affair to anyone except Evelyn. Later they were glad that they had kept the matter secret, for the arrival of the evening papers provided them with additional interesting news. In glancing through the classified section Louise came unexpectedly upon an item which caught her attention.

"Listen to this, Jean!" she said excitedly. " 'Lost or stolen—three valuable dogs. Answer

to names Sally, Hector, Captain. Liberal reward if returned to Warrington Manor.' ''

Jean, taking the paper from her sister's hand,
scanned the advertisement.

"Sally, Hector, Captain," she repeated aloud.
"Well, isn't that wonderful!"

"Now we know where Lettie acquired the
dogs she turned loose in the dormitory. Do you
suppose she deliberately took them from the
estate grounds?"

"I shouldn't be surprised if she did. When
an idea seizes that girl she usually carries it
through, regardless of the consequences," Jean
replied.

"This ad says the dogs are valuable," Louise
went on in a troubled voice. "Someone will
have to notify the Warrington estate."

"Lettie should be the one to do it," Jean said
firmly. "Let's confront her. We'll see what
she has to say!"

CHAPTER IV

AN ACCUSATION

As the Dana girls had fully expected, both Lettie and Ina denied vigorously that they knew anything about the three dogs. Jean rummaged in their wastepaper basket and brought to light the can of dog food. Then their attitude underwent a rapid change, which became one of confusion as the animals' collars were mentioned.

"Oh, you think you're so clever!" Lettie said angrily. "But you can't prove a thing!"

"We've proved it to our own satisfaction at least," retorted Louise. "You must go to Mr. Warrington and tell him what became of the pets."

"Oh, no, I'll not!" Lettie fairly shrieked. "You'll be the one to do it. I had no part in opening the door and allowing those stupid animals to escape. Why, if it hadn't been for you girls, Ina and I could have returned them to the estate and probably collected a nice reward. It was all your fault!"

"I suppose you think the dogs should have remained in this building to bite some of the girls," answered Jean Dana in exasperation. "Why, Mrs. Crandall herself ordered us to drive them out."

"Then you're responsible," Lettie said sullenly. "I'll not take one step toward the Warrington estate. So there!"

"You may compel us to tell the entire story," Louise warned the girl severely.

"All right, tattle! See if I care! I guess you'll soon be in so much trouble yourselves you'll not have time to stir up any for me."

"What do you mean, Lettie?" Jean inquired quickly.

"Oh, I saw you talking with that Zerbe woman," the unpleasant student replied.

"What could that possibly have to do with us getting into trouble?"

"You're pretty stupid not to know. A smart person never would get mixed up with her."

"Just what do you mean?" Jean demanded impatiently of the irritating girl.

"Hm," Lettie replied, "and you call yourselves detectives. Here's a mystery right under your nose and you can't even smell one clue."

As she laughed at her own clever remark, the Danas were a bit abashed. Could it be possible she did know more than they did? They determined to find out.

"Maybe you're right," said Louise, pretending to act resigned. "Of course you know who Mrs. Zerbe is?"

"Indeed I do. Just an old lady who couldn't take care of herself and always sponged on the Warringtons!"

"I guess it must have been hard for her staying alone in the gatehouse," said Jean. "It's probably spooky there after dark."

"Mrs. Zerbe isn't afraid of anything—not a prying old lady like she is," Lettie replied defiantly.

"She seemed very nice to us," the older Dana girl remarked. "I can't imagine her prying into anything. Were there any secrets for her to try to find out?"

"Not at the gatehouse. I didn't mean that. But she tried to know too much of other people's business. So that's why I say you'll get into a lot of trouble pretty soon."

The Danas were so elated to have discovered that Lettie did not know about the secret at the gatehouse they could hardly refrain from smiling. As the girl would say no more, they went to their rooms to discuss the affair privately.

"I'm inclined to think she made up everything she was saying, just to spite us," ventured Jean.

Since Lettie had refused to notify the Warrington estate about the dogs, the girls decided to go there themselves. The following morning the sisters obtained permission to visit the Manor house. Learning of their destination, Professor Crandall offered to drive them there in his car.

"I have an errand at the Cedar Crest Kennels," he explained. "It will not delay me long."

Upon reaching this place, the Danas decided to go inside and look around. As they passed the office, their attention was drawn to a tall, well-dressed gentleman of middle age who was engaged in conversation with the kennel owner.

"Too bad, Mr. Warrington," the latter remarked. "I read in the paper that your Great Dane and Belgian hounds were stolen. You set great store by them too, didn't you?"

"Yes. You see, they belong to my daughter and she will be heartbroken about it when she learns of it," the man answered. "I would give a liberal reward to get them back. I can't figure out how they were stolen, but apparently they were taken in the daytime."

Louise and Jean held a whispered conversation, then stepped forward and introduced themselves, saying they could tell Mr. Warrington what had become of the missing pets.

"I shall be most grateful for any information you can give me," he said courteously, at the same time expressing his astonishment. "Where are the dogs now?"

"We don't know exactly," Louise returned regretfully, "because they escaped from the dormitory at Starhurst School last night. But we do know who took them from your estate."

She went on to relate the entire story, which

was substantiated by Jean. Professor Crandall thought it best to say nothing.

"So Miss Lettie Briggs was responsible," Mr. Warrington commented grimly. "I have never met the young lady but I am well acquainted with her father. We have had several disagreements in business deals, and I frankly say I am not surprised to hear this about his daughter."

It suddenly dawned upon the Danas how Lettie knew Mrs. Zerbe and the reasons for her mean characterization of the old lady.

"I am afraid it was partly our fault that the dogs escaped from the dormitory," Jean said apologetically. "Of course, when we set them free we had no idea of their value."

"I don't blame you in the least. You did right in turning them out, for Captain in particular is unruly when not properly handled. I wonder if I might have a talk with this Briggs girl?"

"Certainly, Mr. Warrington," replied Professor Crandall. "Will you come back to the school with us?"

The estate owner glanced at his watch. "Thank you, but I have an appointment in fifteen minutes. My daughter Evangeline is arriving at Penfield on the eleven o'clock train and I want to meet her. However, we'll both be glad to drive over to your school a little later."

"Any time at all, Mr. Warrington."

"Shall we make it eleven-thirty then?" the owner of the Manor house proposed briskly.

When it was learned at the dormitory that the famous Mr. Warrington and his beautiful daughter soon would arrive, the news was received with mingled feelings. Some of the students were curious to see a man who was under investigation, others to get a close view of the heiress whose picture appeared so often in newspapers and in magazines.

Ina and Lettie had some misgivings. Their uneasiness increased when the Crandalls sent for them to appear in the office, where Jean and Louise already were waiting.

Promptly at half past eleven a black limousine rolled up to the building. Mr. Warrington alighted and assisted his daughter, a young woman of about twenty-one who wore a smartly cut fur jacket made of sable skins. The girl was as charming as she was attractive-looking, and as she tripped lightly toward the head-mistress's office many eyes followed her admiringly, for she smiled pleasantly at the students.

"Jean and Louise are lucky," Evelyn Starr murmured, "having a chance to meet such a person."

"So will Lettie and Ina," added a classmate with a laugh. "But I'm glad not to be in *their* shoes right now!"

Inside the office the culprits were having an

uncomfortable half hour. Terrified at being confronted by Richard Warrington, they tried in every way to shift the blame from themselves.

"Probably Louise and Jean Dana stole the dogs from the estate to get a reward," the Briggs girl said defiantly. "I saw them walking through the fields on the very day the animals appeared here at the dormitory."

Obviously the remark was made in the hope that she could save herself from punishment. To the intense relief of Jean and Louise, neither Mr. Warrington nor his daughter Evangeline seemed to place much faith in the false accusation.

"We shall say nothing more about the matter," the young woman declared at last. "You can readily see that while the money loss is considerable I am not thinking about that. Sally, a Great Dane, has won many ribbons. Father and I raised all three dogs from the time they were puppies, and we love them."

"Isn't there a chance the pets may return to the estate?" Louise asked hopefully.

"It is possible they will find their way back," replied Miss Warrington, speaking without conviction.

At that moment the conference was interrupted by a school messenger who apologetically came to the door of the office and said that Mr. Warrington was wanted outside.

"A detective to see you, sir," were the man's startling words.

Quickly the caller arose from his chair. His daughter looked distressed.

"Oh, Father," she murmured anxiously. "Do you suppose it's about the investigation——"

"Never mind," broke in Mr. Warrington. "I'll see the man at once."

Turning to Professor and Mrs. Crandall he thanked them for their assistance. With a friendly smile directed at Jean and Louise he escorted his daughter hurriedly from the office. Joining a man who waited outside, they quickly drove away in the limousine.

"I liked Miss Warrington, didn't you, Louise?" Jean asked after she and her sister had left the office. "Not spoiled a bit."

"Yes, she is very attractive."

"I didn't think so," spoke up Lettie Briggs in a harsh voice. She was standing near them, watching the departing car. "She acted too know-it-all. And did you see how nervous she got when the detective arrived!"

"Perhaps you imagined it," replied Jean, although mentally she had made the same observation herself.

"Oh, no, I didn't. Mark my words, Richard Warrington will be in prison before another month rolls around. My father says so!"

To the annoyance of the Danas, Lettie told nearly everyone in the dormitory that Miss Warrington was a very arrogant, conceited young woman, the daughter of a man who would face a prison sentence soon. While most of the students knew the Briggs girl well enough to discount her remarks, there were some who actually believed them.

Saturday afternoon found Louise and Jean with time on their hands. With a great desire to learn if the Warringtons had recovered the three missing dogs, they hiked to the estate where they presented themselves at the main entrance. The gates were closed, but as they jingled a little bell a short, stocky man came from the stone gatehouse. They immediately guessed, and correctly so, that he was the new attendant, Bert Badger.

"Good afternoon," said Jean pleasantly. "Will you open the gate for us, please?"

The man peered at them doubtfully. "Well, I don't know," he said. "Are the Warringtons expecting you?"

"No," replied Jean, "we merely came to inquire if their missing dogs have been recovered."

"I can tell you that myself. They haven't come home yet."

"Oh, that's too bad," murmured Louise in disappointment. "I thought surely they would return of their own accord."

As Bert Badger still made no move to unlock the gate, Jean said, "I should like to talk with Miss Warrington."

"I'll have to telephone her and ask. Can't let you in without permission."

The Danas gave their names, waiting while the man disappeared into the little stone house. The place did not look in the least mysterious. What was the secret it held, was the thought going through the minds of the girls.

"Sorry to have kept you so long," the man apologized when he returned. He swung wide the gate. "You're to go to the main house."

Jean and Louise passed through. Beyond, as far as they could see, stretched a velvety lawn, still green despite the lateness of the season. The grounds were landscaped beautifully and through the trees they caught glimpses of fountains and a withered rose garden.

"Isn't it gorgeous—" Louise began, but her words ended in a gasp.

Unexpectedly she was struck from behind just above the level of her knees. Losing her balance she toppled over and was trampled by a huge hound which raced past her toward the mansion.

"Are you hurt?" Jean cried, turning to help her sister get up.

"Not a bit," Louise laughed. "But that dog took me by surprise. Where did he come from?"

"Through the open gate."

As Jean spoke, a second Belgian hound dashed toward the girls, racing after the other dog.

"Why, I believe that is either Hector or Captain!" exclaimed Louise. "They look exactly like the pets we chased from the dormitory."

At that moment Mr. Warrington appeared on the veranda of the mansion. The two animals rushed straight toward him. Leaping up on him, they tried to lick his face.

"Hector! Captain! How did you get back home?" the man laughed. "Eve will be so glad to see you!"

Then his gaze fell upon Louise and Jean who were walking slowly toward the porch.

"You brought the dogs?" he inquired in a surprised tone.

"Oh, no," responded Jean. "When the gate was thrown open they bolted in behind us."

"I see," said Mr. Warrington. "The dogs *followed* you here?" he added, wonder in his voice.

"Not to our knowledge," replied Louise hastily.

The man seemed puzzled at the explanation.

"It was merely accidental that they came home just as we arrived," said Jean earnestly after the barking pets had been taken to their kennels by a gardener. "Mr. Warrington, the story we told you at school is true."

"Suppose you come inside," suggested the

man. "We'll talk it over in there. My lawyer, Mr. Hinkley, is here. I'll have him discuss the matter of a reward with you," he added simply.

The handsome executive led the way inside. The Danas followed, realizing they were in an awkward situation.

CHAPTER V

A Bold Reporter

ALTHOUGH they felt deeply chagrined by the
turn of events, Jean and Louise followed
Mr. Warrington into the mansion as they still
wanted to see his daughter. They were escorted
down a long, beautifully furnished hall to a library which was lined with shelves of books. A
distinguished looking, middle-aged man who
proved to be the lawyer, Mr. Hinkley, arose as
they entered and was introduced to the girls.

"Well, now," he said to the Danas, after the
situation had been explained to him, "I have no
idea how much to offer you for the return of the
dogs. Would a hundred dollars do?"

"We are not looking for any reward," declared Jean spiritedly.

"And we wouldn't accept any," added Louise.
"My sister and I never were more surprised
in our lives than when those dogs followed us
through the gate. They must have been close
to the estate, waiting for a chance to get inside."

Mr. Hinkley thereupon asked the girls several
questions but could not shake their story that
they knew nothing about how the pets had escaped from the Manor nor why they had returned. As the Danas were wondering what

the outcome would be, the conversation was interrupted by the arrival of a servant.

"Mrs. Zerbe to see you, sir," he said to Mr. Warrington.

"Oh, yes, I was expecting her," replied the owner of the mansion. "Show her in at once."

The man glanced significantly at his lawyer, plainly inferring that he should conclude his business with the callers without further delay.

"I believe that will be all, for the time being at least," said Mr. Hinkley, rising. "Your story seems logical. At least we shall give you the benefit of the doubt. Shall I show you to the door?"

Jean and Louise, stepping into the hall, came face to face with Mrs. Zerbe. The woman failed to recognize them until they spoke her name.

"Oh, how do you do?" she murmured nervously. "I—I didn't know you for a moment. It is rather dark here in the house and I haven't my glasses on. I can't see well without them."

Mr. Warrington stood in the doorway of the library, frowning.

"I didn't know that you young ladies were acquainted with Mrs. Zerbe," he said somewhat dubiously.

"We met only the other day," the old lady replied quickly before the Dana girls could speak.

Since the woman so obviously feared that they might betray her, Louise and Jean did not distress her by lingering to talk. As they went down the hall they heard Mr. Warrington ask in a low tone not intended for their ears:

"Just where did you meet those two girls, Mrs. Zerbe?"

"It was while they were hiking near the estate," the old lady answered evasively. "A very casual meeting, I assure you, Mr. Warrington. You have nothing to fear."

After Mr. Hinkley had ushered the girls out the front door they did not immediately leave the estate. Instead, they wandered about the gardens, inspecting the swimming pool, and the orchard adjoining the service section of the house.

"I wonder if Mrs. Zerbe will tell Mr. Warrington that we read the note he sent her?" Jean mused as they walked along slowly.

"You may be sure she won't," replied her sister. "She is too afraid that he might censure her for letting us see it."

"I wish we could visit the gatehouse while we're here," Jean declared impulsively. "That note made me curious."

"Bert Badger would be suspicious if we should try to get inside. We can't afford to make any more false moves around this place," Louise laughed.

"I suppose you're right," Jean agreed. "We'll never learn anything if we get into difficulties with Mr. Warrington."

The two girls paused beneath a giant maple tree which stood close to the mansion. Hearing a rustle of leaves, Louise glanced upward. Then her eyes wandered toward another tree not far away where a breeze seemed to stir the foliage.

"That's funny," she murmured, half to herself. "No wind blowing."

To Jean's surprise her sister walked to the trunk and peered into the boughs. Gazing upward, she looked straight into the eyes of a young man with a camera and a flashlight outfit.

"Sh! Don't give me away," he said, irritated.

"Who are you?" Louise inquired curiously. "What are you doing up there?"

"Picking cherries," he retorted coolly. "Name's Abe Mantel from the Penfield *Post*. Now will you go away before you bring out the servants to chase me?"

"Why are you spying on the Warringtons?" queried Jean.

"Because it's my assignment," the fellow replied calmly. "I want to get a picture of Warrington and his lawyer for my sheet."

As Jean and Louise both knew, the Penfield *Post* was a tabloid newspaper which had not been in existence long. The publisher, a man of questionable ethics, was hoping to build up a large circulation by printing sensational pictures and news stories.

"I don't see why we should go away," Louise

said firmly. "In fact, I think we ought to call Mr. Warrington."

"You'll be sorry if you do," the reporter warned her. "You two may find yourselves in flashing headlines if you do."

"You can't intimidate us by such threats," returned Jean. "Take as many pictures of us as you like."

"I've already done so. I snapped one as you came through the gate, followed by those two dogs. That was a good one," he laughed.

Jean and Louise glanced quickly at each other. It was against school rules for students' photos to be in the paper without the consent of the headmistress. Furthermore, the Danas realized that if such a picture should be printed many persons would assume they had been in possession of the stolen hounds.

"I don't see what good such a thing would do you," Jean said, hoping to talk the man out of using the snap. "Why don't you let us have the film?"

"Oh, no! Never can tell when you may break into print. Then it will come in handy. You might decide to rob a bank one of these days," he laughed. "Then I'd have the picture ready to use."

"My, but you think a long way ahead," Louise said ironically.

"That's me," he answered. "Now will you please go away from here? Listen, run along like nice little girlies and I'll give you a treat. How would you like dinner and a dance?''

"That's not our idea of a treat," returned Jean. "If you would give us that picture you took of us we might be able to come to terms."

"Nothing doing," the reporter declined. "I couldn't give you the film even if I should want to. You see, it's on the roll and I still have another picture to take."

At that moment a limousine drew up to the doorway of the mansion. Mr. Warrington and Mrs. Zerbe, evidently intending to drive away together, stepped out onto the porch. Mantel held his camera ready.

"Don't snap that!" cried Louise.

The Danas called out a warning to the couple, but were too late. They heard a clicking sound from overhead.

"Got it!" chuckled the reporter.

Quickly he began to wind the used film through his camera. So interested was he in his work that he became careless of his position. As he removed the roll from the box he suddenly lost his balance.

"Help!" he called frantically, clutching for the nearest tree bough.

Fortunately for the reporter, Mr. Warrington and Mrs. Zerbe did not hear him for they had entered the car and driven away. In an ungainly heap Abe Mantel tumbled almost at the feet of the Dana girls. His camera fell from his

hand and the roll of pictures bounded away.
Quick as a flash Louise darted forward and
seized the film.

"Hey, drop that!" angrily shouted the reporter who had not been hurt by the fall.

"Run, Louise!" advised Jean.

Together the girls raced down the driveway
toward the gatehouse. When they glanced back
over their shoulders they could not see the man
anywhere.

"What became of him, do you suppose?" Jean
demanded, pausing. "I thought he would follow and catch us at the gate!"

"He was too shrewd for that," returned
Louise. "He'll find a new hiding place and wait
for Mr. Warrington to return. Then he'll snap
another picture."

"We'll have to warn the watchman."

"Yes," nodded Louise. "Let's tell the lodge-
keeper right away."

Hurrying to the gatehouse, they found Bert
Badger who had just let Mr. Warrington's car
out of the estate. Learning of the intruder, he
rushed into the stone building and pressed a
button which sounded an alarm.

Almost at once servants and gardeners began
to appear. Everyone conducted an intensive
search for the elusive reporter. Suddenly Jean
caught a glimpse of the man hiding in the rose
arbor.

"There he is!" she called.

CHAPTER VI

The Extra Key

"Halt!" shouted Bert Badger.

As servants pursued the reporter, he ran toward the main gate. Realizing he would be caught, Abe Mantel swerved aside and hastened toward another exit.

"This may go on for half an hour, Jean," Louise said to her sister. "We're not needed any longer, so suppose we slip away. We have the film. Let's hurry away with it."

"Yes, it's getting late and we should be back at the dormitory," nodded Jean, reaching up to unfasten the gate.

The girls ran much of the distance to Starhurst. Even so, it was five minutes after six when they reached the school. The dinner gong had sounded and the meal was being served as they slid into their places as inconspicuously as possible.

Their late arrival would have gone unobserved by Mrs. Crandall, had not Lettie Briggs called attention to it. In a loud voice she said:

"Another minute and the doors would have been closed. You girls must have spent the afternoon at a moving picture show. Or did you go on another hike?"

47

"These nice fall days soon will be gone," Louise replied evasively. "One must make the most of them, you know."

"You and Jean certainly do," Lettie declared with a sniff. "I'll venture to say you went to the Warrington estate."

"For once your guess is correct," Jean said pleasantly. "And we have some very good news for you. Two of Miss Warrington's dogs have returned home."

An expression of obvious relief crossed Lettie's face, but it was gone in an instant.

"Why should that be good news for me?" she demanded aloofly. "It wasn't my fault the dogs vanished. You and Louise are the ones to blame for their disappearance in the beginning."

"You're not very grateful, it seems to me," responded Louise, losing patience. "Since that's the way you feel about it, there is no need for us to give Mrs. Crandall the information."

Lettie's attitude changed instantly.

"I was only joking," she said hastily. "Mrs. Crandall has been blaming me. If she hears the dogs are back again she may forget about the whole affair."

"And you may escape being expelled," spoke up a student across the table. "Really, Lettie, you don't seem to recognize friendly help when it is given to you."

After dinner Louise and Jean made their report to Mrs. Crandall, for they wished to be absolutely fair about everything. The headmistress expressed relief that the Warringtons would not suffer any great loss and assured the Dana girls she would not expel Lettie Briggs for the prank.

"It was done thoughtlessly," she declared, "and Lettie already has told me that she is sorry."

The next day Lettie and Ina Mason kept to themselves. They speculated a great deal upon the association of the Dana girls with the Warringtons and later ventured to ask many direct questions of them.

"All right, keep it to yourself!" Lettie said irritably as Jean gave the girl an evasive reply to an inquiry that evening. "I guess I know something you would like to hear. It concerns a certain reporter named Abe Mantel."

Lettie would say no more, but Ina was less secretive. She openly boasted that her roommate had managed to gain entrance to the Warrington estate and had been aided by the newspaper man in doing so.

"I wish we could learn more about that," Jean remarked to her sister later. "I'm sure Bert Badger did not allow either of them to pass through the gate."

"Lettie will not tell what happened unless we force her to do so," replied Louise.

"How can we? I haven't a single idea," sighed her sister.

"We'll have to give the problem a little serious thought," laughed the older girl.

The next day classes were dismissed early so that the students who wished might attend a basketball game between two rival teams, the Reds and the Blues. Neither Louise nor Jean was playing. Furthermore Lettie, because of a misdemeanor, had been told to stay in her room. This gave the Danas their looked-for opportunity.

"I believe we're the only persons who aren't attending the game," Jean remarked about two o'clock, when the dormitory practically was deserted.

"It's a splendid time to make Lettie talk!" said Louise.

"Suppose we try it."

Hurrying down the deserted hall the girls reached Lettie's room. They peered through the door which stood slightly ajar.

"I don't believe she is here—" Jean began, only to lapse into silence as Louise gave her a warning nudge.

The Briggs girl could be seen in the wardrobe closet rummaging about for something which had been covered up in the general disorder.

"Let's lock her in," whispered Louise. "Then I'll bet she'll talk!"

"We'll only frighten her," agreed Jean.

Tiptoeing into the room, the girls quickly

slammed shut the closet door. The prisoner
gave a terrified scream and began to beat upon
the panel with her fists.

"Let me out! Let me out!"

"All in good time, Lettie," chuckled Louise.
"Suppose we have a little chat first. Would
you mind telling us how you and Abe Mantel
managed to get into the grounds of the Warrington estate?"

"I won't tell you a thing! Let me out! Let
me out! I'm smothering!"

"You're not smothering yet," said Jean
coolly, "but you might if we should leave you
here and go away."

"You don't dare!" cried Lettie. "I'll scream
for help!"

"Scream all you like," said Louise pleasantly.
"No one besides ourselves is in the building."

Lettie remained very quiet for a moment.
Then she demanded sullenly:

"What do you want of me?"

"We just told you," said Jean. "Only a little
information. Where did you first meet the reporter Abe Mantel?"

"Out near the Warrington estate," Lettie
answered grudgingly.

"What were you doing there?"

"I was taking a walk. I guess I have a right
to walk where I please!"

"To be sure," said Jean soothingly. "I im-

agine you and Abe Mantel were two persons
with but a single thought. You both wanted to
get inside the Warrington estate.''

"We did, too!" Lettie retorted.

"How?" asked Louise patiently.

"I'll not tell you."

"Very well. Jean, I guess we may as well
return to our suite."

"No, wait," Lettie called in panic. "I'll tell
you. Abe had a key to the gate."

"A key!" Jean exclaimed. "Where did he
get it, I wonder?"

"How should I know?" Lettie asked crossly.
"I didn't ask him a lot of silly questions. Now
I've told you all I know so let me out of here!"

Louise obligingly unlocked the door and the
angry girl stumbled forth into the light.

"I have a notion to report you for this trick!"
she stormed. "It's downright cruelty."

Louise and Jean could tell by Lettie's manner
that she would not report them to Mrs. Crandall. While they had acted in a somewhat high-
handed way, no other tactics would have
achieved the same result.

"Thanks for the information," Jean said
with a laugh as she and Louise turned away.

Eager to pass along what they had just
learned, the Dana girls walked to the Warrington estate. The day was a bright one, belying
the lateness of the season. Although Thanks-

giving was not far away, as yet there had been only one light frost.

"This weather can't last much longer," sighed Louise as they tramped along. "Once it turns cold we'll not be able to make so many excursions."

Reaching the front gate of the beautiful grounds, the girls found Bert Badger in attendance as usual.

"I don't know about letting you in," he said doubtfully. "Mr. Warrington spoke to me very severely for what happened the other day."

"It wasn't your fault that reporter managed to get into the grounds," Louise returned.

"Mr. Warrington seemed to think I admitted him through the gate. He says if anything like that happens again I'll lose my job. Maybe I will anyway."

"Did the man get away?" inquired Jean. "Didn't you catch him?"

The gatekeeper shook his head. "He was a spry fellow. Climbed a tree and scrambled over the wall. He couldn't have got in that way though."

"We know how he did it," Louise revealed. "That's what we came to tell you. The man had a key to the gate."

"He did!" exclaimed Bert Badger. "Well, then that excuses me! Say, I'm mighty grateful for the information."

As a limousine swung up to the gate from the main highway, Louise and Jean quickly stepped aside. Mr. Warrington in the back seat recognized them.

"Good afternoon," he said in a cheerful voice. "Beautiful day."

Relieved that the man seemed to bear them no ill feeling, the Dana girls returned the greeting and came closer to the car.

"We have information that may interest you, Mr. Warrington," Louise said, repeating what she previously had told Badger.

"I'll look into the matter at once," the mansion owner promised. "I can't understand how this Abe Mantel obtained a key. I admit I thought my gatekeeper had let him in."

"Oh, no, sir," protested Badger.

"This clears you," Mr. Warrington told the servant. "I am very glad to learn the truth."

Before the car could drive through the gate, Jean ventured to ask Mr. Warrington if he could provide her with Mrs. Zerbe's present address.

"Louise and I thought we might call on her some day," she added in as casual a manner as she could assume.

Mr. Warrington hesitated, obviously not wishing to give the requested information.

"Now let me see," he pretended to muse. "Where did Mrs. Zerbe say she was living? I don't seem to recall at the moment."

The Danas were not to be deceived. They understood perfectly well that the man was afraid to have them communicate with the woman lest they learn too much about his personal affairs.

"Never mind," said Jean, to ease an awkward situation. "It isn't of great importance."

"Well, glad to have met you again," returned Mr. Warrington, obviously relieved.

He signaled to the chauffeur and the car rolled on through the gate.

"At least we did Badger a good turn," Jean remarked as the girls trudged toward the dormitory. "Isn't it funny how fearful Mr. Warrington is that we'll learn too much?"

"His attitude only makes me more curious—and suspicious," replied her sister.

"I wonder if the secret is entirely a personal one or of a nature the authorities would like to get hold of," said Jean.

The late afternoon mail had arrived when the girls reached the dormitory. They paused at the box in the hall and were delighted to find a thick letter from Aunt Harriet. The envelope was addressed to both girls, but Jean seized upon it first. After skimming over the first paragraph, she gave a low cry of astonishment.

"Here is real news, Louise! Read this and I think you'll decide that we may be able to make a most profitable use of our holiday trip to Oak Falls!"

CHAPTER VII

Ruined Costumes

"What does Aunt Harriet write?" inquired Louise eagerly.

"First of all, Uncle Ned will be home for Thanksgiving," revealed Jean, "though that's not the startling news. Aunt Harriet says that Mrs. Borden who lives on our street in Oak Falls has a new boarder."

"What is so exciting about that?" demanded Louise a trifle impatiently.

"Wait until I tell you the boarder's name. It's Mrs. Zerbe!"

"Mrs. Henry Zerbe?" Louise gasped.

"She doesn't say, but it must be the same person. Zerbe is such an uncommon name."

"Then Mrs. Zerbe must have fled from Penfield to Oak Falls, where she thought no one would know her!" exclaimed her sister.

"It looks that way," nodded Jean as she offered the letter to her sister. "This is a good joke on Mr. Warrington. He wouldn't tell us where the old lady had gone and now we know."

"It could be another Mrs. Zerbe."

"Yes, though it's not likely, Louise. Aunt

56

Harriet writes that the new boarder is an old lady who arrived from out of town only a day ago,'' offered Jean.

"Then it must be the same woman! Everything fits. During the holidays perhaps we'll be able to get well acquainted with her.''

"And learn more about Mr. Warrington's secret!'' laughed Jean in high good humor. "Oh, I can't wait now for Thanksgiving to come!''

"A play to be given too,'' sighed Louise. "That reminds me, we're supposed to press all the costumes. A nice job!''

"It won't take us long once we start. Evelyn promised she would help us.''

"Let's find her right after dinner and get the work out of the way. Tomorrow we'll have no time,'' said Louise wisely.

She and Jean had been assigned leading parts in a one-act playlet, a skit of early American life which was to be given the following evening in the school auditorium. For weeks the girls had rehearsed and used their spare time making Puritan costumes. Mrs. Crandall had requested the Danas to assume the task of pressing the dresses.

After locating Evelyn, the girls carried the pile of costumes to the dormitory laundry. There they hooked up three separate electric irons and started their tedious task. Evelyn laid her group at the end of her ironing board, one on top of the other. Then she started to press a blouse. Suddenly a bell in the basement began to clang.

"The fire alarm!" cried Jean. "This is a funny time to have a drill."

"Maybe there is a fire!" Louise exclaimed.

She and Jean unsnapped their irons and with Evelyn rushed for the stairway. Along with the other students they ran from the building.

"Where is the fire?" one of them asked.

"I don't see any smoke," said Louise.

After a long wait in the chilly courtyard the students were informed by Professor Crandall that the alarm had been a mistake. In cleaning one of the hallways the janitor had pressed the control switch accidentally.

The students filed back into the building. Evelyn, Jean and Louise started for the basement laundry room.

"Say, maybe that wasn't a false alarm after all," Jean declared, pausing to sniff the air. "I smell something burning."

"So do I," declared Louise anxiously. "It couldn't be from our irons because we turned off the current."

"I didn't," wailed Evelyn. "Oh, dear, I forgot. Do you suppose——"

Quickly the three girls ran to the laundry. One glance at Evelyn's ironing board disclosed a pile of smoking garments. The hot iron had turned its way through almost every costume.

Jean darted forward to rescue the clothing, but a great deal of damage already had been done.

"Oh, the costumes are ruined," moaned Evelyn, jerking the electric cord from the wall. "How could I have been so careless?"

Although Louise and Jean did not blame their friend aloud, they felt sick at heart as they surveyed the situation. Every garment except one had been burned and the holes were large ones.

"With the play scheduled for tomorrow night there will be no time to make new dresses," Evelyn said gloomily.

"Maybe these can be mended," Louise offered hopefully.

While the Dana girls were placing a new cover on the ironing board, Lettie Briggs sauntered into the laundry to press one of her frocks. As this was unusual, the girls figured she had found an excuse to learn what they were doing. Instantly she noted what had happened. Since she had been unable to get a part in the play herself, she could not hide her satisfaction at the disaster.

"Now you've done it!" she gloated. "Wait until Mrs. Crandall learns about this! She'll probably deprive you girls of your vacations."

"It was all my fault," declared Evelyn honestly. "I shall take all the blame myself."

"Jean and Louise are responsible for the costumes being ready,'' said Lettie airily. ''Mrs. Crandall didn't tell them to ask for any assistance. Oh, they'll catch it all right!''

After the unpleasant girl had gone, the three chums went contritely to the headmistress and told her their story. They could not blame her for speaking severely to them, for in addition to nearly causing a fire they had all but ruined the chances of producing the play.

''I think we can mend the dresses so they won't look too bad,'' Louise told the woman. ''At least we'll try.''

Late into the evening Evelyn and the Dana girls sewed frantically. Other friends came to help them. Just before the lights-out bell sounded the last garment was finished.

''You can tell they've been mended,'' Evelyn said in a discouraged voice, ''but they look better than I expected they would.''

''The Puritans were poor people,'' declared Louise, trying to be optimistic in spite of everything. ''They must have worn patched clothing in those days. The costumes look more realistic now.''

''I only hope Mrs. Crandall thinks so,'' sighed Evelyn.

The following evening the play was given. Under the soft glow of the lights there were few persons in the audience who could tell that the garments had been repaired extensively. Jean and Louise played their parts unusually well. At the conclusion Mrs. Crandall came back stage and praised them for their excellent acting. Nothing was said about the condition of the Puritan attire.

"I guess everything looked all right," Jean said in relief after the headmistress had left. "We can enjoy our Thanksgiving at home after all."

"Won't Lettie and Ina be disappointed!" laughed Louise as she wiped make-up from her face. "They were almost certain we would lose our privilege of going away."

Wednesday afternoon found the Danas on the train bound for home. They were the first passengers off at Oak Falls and looked about them eagerly for their Aunt Harriet.

"I guess she decided not to meet us at the train," Jean remarked. "But there's someone we know—Mrs. Borden. Our neighbor."

"Why, how do you do, Louise and Jean?" she greeted the girls cordially. "Your aunt said you were coming. For a week she has been cooking good things to eat!"

"We'll do justice to them," laughed Louise. "Boarding school food grows monotonous after one has had it for weeks at a time. What is this we hear about you, Mrs. Borden? Aunt Harriet writes you have a new boarder."

"Yes, she came a few days ago; a Mrs. Zerbe, and as nice a person as I've ever had in my home. But she may leave any time."

"Doesn't she like Oak Falls?" Jean asked the woman quickly.

"She seems to. It's because of that man who keeps annoying her, I think."

"What man do you mean? Not anyone here in Oak Falls?" asked Louise.

"Oh, no, if I knew the fellow I'd soon put a stop to it! I never set eyes on him before he came to the house. The day after Mrs. Zerbe arrived he called and he has been here twice since."

"What does he look like, Mrs. Borden?" Louise inquired thoughtfully.

"I suppose one might call him good-looking," the woman replied grudgingly. "He has black, curly hair and rather bold manners. It upsets Mrs. Zerbe when he talks to her. She said this morning she might decide to leave, and I suspect he is the reason."

The description struck both Louise and Jean as vaguely familiar, but they did not reveal their thoughts. Instead, they expressed sympathy for Mrs. Borden, who always seemed to have trouble in keeping her rooms occupied.

"I shouldn't like to lose Mrs. Zerbe as a boarder," the woman said with a sigh. "Perhaps you girls could do something to help get rid of that man."

"We might at that," laughed Jean. "You see, we already have an idea that we know Mrs. Zerbe. Tell us a little more about her."

"Well, I should say she is at least seventy-five. When she came she seemed strong and well, but the past two days I have noticed that she looks pale. I suggested calling in Doctor Bailey but Mrs. Zerbe wouldn't consent. She has opinions of her own," the boarding-house mistress smiled.

"She must be the same Mrs. Zerbe we know," declared Louise, nodding her head. "We met the woman at Penfield a few days ago."

"Then perhaps you are acquainted with the stranger who has been annoying her?"

"We may have met him but we aren't sure. I wish we could see him," said Jean.

"Usually he comes to call in the morning. Tomorrow why don't you and Louise drop over and pay me a friendly call?" their neighbor suggested. "Stay for a time and perhaps he'll arrive while you are at the house."

"We'll do it!" Jean promised eagerly.

"I feel Mrs. Zerbe should not hear any news which might tend to excite her," said Mrs. Borden. "I wish she would consult a doctor," continued the woman with a sigh. "I wouldn't want anything tragic to happen to her in my house."

CHAPTER VIII

The Strange Visitor

After the woman had left them, Jean and Louise checked their suitcases in the station and walked slowly toward home.

"I hope Mrs. Zerbe isn't seriously ill," Louise remarked anxiously. "At seventy-five one doesn't throw off a disease easily."

"You're right," admitted Jean. "If anything should happen to her I wonder how Mr. Warrington would take it?"

A few minutes later as Jean and Louise reached the Dana home, their aunt met them at the front door. After giving each of her nieces an affectionate kiss, she led the way into the living room.

"My, but it's good to be home!" exclaimed Jean, her eyes sparkling like jewels.

"I've been waiting for this a long, long time," said Louise. "Home, sweet home again."

"I intended to meet your train," said her aunt, "but at the last minute I was delayed. Cora dropped a box of eggs on the floor, so I had to attend to the oven while she went to the store after another dozen."

"Applecore seems to be running true to

form," Jean laughed, sniffing the air. "My, do I smell good things cooking?"

"Mince pies for tomorrow's dinner. I only hope Cora doesn't ruin them!" laughed Aunt Harriet.

Miss Dana lowered her voice as a noisy shuffling of feet warned her that the maid was approaching. Cora Appel greeted the Dana girls warmly and lingered to talk to them.

"Applecore, I think I smell something burning," Jean presently remarked.

"Oh my, it must be the marshmallow pudding!" exclaimed the maid, starting for the kitchen. "I forgot about it and left it boilin' on the stove!"

Miss Dana sighed and shook her head. "Cora is a dreadful trial," she confessed in a low voice. "Still, I should miss her if she were to leave."

"Her mistakes enliven the household at least," laughed Jean. "Oh, by the way, when will Uncle Ned get here?"

Miss Dana glanced at the mantel clock. "Very soon. He is coming on the five-thirty train."

"Let's meet him," proposed Louise to her sister.

"We'll just have time to get there," said Jean instantly. "We can take the car and pick up our bags."

By hurrying the girls reached the railroad station a few minutes before the train came in.

Captain Dana, trim and distinguished-looking, was one of the first passengers to alight from the coaches.

"Ahoy there," he waved to his nieces. "I thought you might be here to pilot me safely into the home port."

"How is everything on the *Balaska?*" inquired Louise as the three started for home, crowding together on the front seat.

"Splendid," the captain declared. "We had a little labor trouble during our last voyage. Nothing of consequence."

"I suppose you've read about Mr. Warrington's difficulties with the government," Louise went on. "Isn't he the man who is president of the steamship company which owns the *Balaska?*"

"Yes," admitted Captain Dana, his face becoming serious. "I've been wondering how the case will come out. I'm fairly well acquainted with Mr. Warrington. He seems to be a fine man."

"You know him, Uncle Ned?" Jean inquired eagerly.

"Aye, he often travels on my ship. Usually he and his valet, Nat Kaner, engage our best suite. Now there's a rascal for you, if I'm any judge of character."

"Not Mr. Warrington?" questioned Louise quickly.

"No, his valet Kaner. I venture to say Mr.

Warrington's troubles are caused in part by that fellow having a hand in his business affairs. The funny thing is he trusts this servant implicitly."

"Why do you say that, Uncle Ned?" asked Jean curiously.

"Kaner is a schemer, out to get all he can for himself. Why, on one of our recent trips to Europe, Mr. Warrington made a bitter complaint about being charged for extra services. Later I made a careful investigation and discovered that Kaner had been running heavy bills in his employer's name, all the while purchasing the various items for himself."

"Didn't you tell Mr. Warrington about it?" Louise inquired.

"I haven't seen him since. However, I may not say anything to him. He has great faith in Kaner and might doubt my word. He sometimes gives important errands to the man as he would to a secretary."

Louise and Jean related what they had heard regarding the multi-millionaire and were pleased that Captain Dana seemed deeply interested in their story.

"It might be advisable for you to cultivate Mrs. Zerbe," he said, a twinkle in his eye. "If you should learn her secret, pass it on to me!"

The next morning while their Aunt Harriet and Cora Appel were busy with preparations for the Thanksgiving dinner, Jean and Louise

went to the Borden home. They rang the doorbell several times but got no response.

"This is strange," remarked Louise.

The girls were about to leave when the
boarding-house mistress came to admit them.

"I'm sorry to have kept you waiting," she
apologized. "I was upstairs following the doctor's orders and I couldn't come right away."

"The doctor?" asked Jean in surprise.
"Then Mrs. Zerbe finally decided to call him?"

Mrs. Borden shook her head. "I decided to,
and it's lucky I did. Mrs. Zerbe is in bed this
morning, a very sick woman according to the
physician."

"Not seriously ill?" Louise questioned her
uneasily, fearing the worst.

"A heart attack. And you know what that
might mean at her age."

"Oh," gasped Jean, stunned by the information. "You don't mean she'll die?"

"Only a miracle can save her. The doctor
says she may linger two or three days or she
may go quickly. We've sent for a nurse."

"Poor Mrs. Zerbe," Louise said sadly. "I
suppose she has no living relatives."

"None to my knowledge. Her only close
friend seems to be a Mr. Warrington."

"He was her employer," explained Louise.
"Could Jean and I see Mrs. Zerbe?"

"I guess it will be all right, since you know
her," was the reply. "But don't stay long."

Although the Danas expected to see the patient wan and ill looking, they were not prepared for the shock they received. The old lady showed plainly that she was suffering not only physically but mentally. On the sunken face was the most pathetic expression imaginable.

"Mrs. Zerbe, I am Louise Dana," said the older girl when the woman, staring straight ahead, did not notice the callers. "My sister and I met you in Penfield."

"Don't try to talk," advised Jean. "We live near here, so we came over to see you."

At last the faintest flicker of a smile could be seen on the lined face.

"I'm—glad—you—came," whispered Mrs. Zerbe with difficulty. "After I—go," there was a long pause, "take things—to—Warr——"

Unable to go on, the little woman closed her eyes. Louise gently held the feverish hands, while Jean applied cooling wet cloths to the patient's forehead. After a few minutes of rest, the old lady opened her eyes again.

"You want us to get in touch with Mr. Warrington?" the older girl asked.

The feeble figure nodded her head very slightly. "Books—letters," she whispered. "Good—girls. No one else—must—get——"

Again she lapsed into sleep. Mrs. Borden, coming in, said that the doctor was arriving, so the girls left the house.

The news of Mrs. Zerbe's serious illness served to detract from the gaiety of an otherwise happy Thanksgiving at the Dana home. In the late afternoon Louise and Jean returned once more to the rooming house in the company of their aunt.

"You are very kind to come," said Mrs. Borden, "but there is nothing anyone can do now. Poor Mrs. Zerbe passed away half an hour ago. She died peacefully and was in no pain."

Shocked by the news, the sisters sent a telegram to Mr. Warrington, informing him of what had happened. Two days later they attended the funeral with a small number of neighbors. Mr. Warrington did not come to Oak Falls; nor was any word received from relatives or acquaintances of the deceased woman.

"I don't know what to do with Mrs. Zerbe's personal belongings," Mrs. Borden said anxiously to the Dana girls. "I suppose they should be turned over to Mr. Warrington."

"Jean and I will take them to him when we return to Penfield," Louise offered helpfully. "Mrs. Zerbe asked us to see that he got them."

"We'll go to her room now and help you pack the things," said Jean.

"That won't take long. Mrs. Zerbe had very little clothing with her."

The Dana girls accompanied the woman upstairs. They had just finished packing the wearing apparel, a few books and some letters into the three bags Mrs. Zerbe had brought, when a knock was heard on the front door. Peering out a window, Mrs. Borden saw a tall, good-looking, red-haired man in a derby hat.

"I've never seen him before," she said to the girls. "He doesn't look like an agent, either."

Mrs. Borden hastened to the door, followed by the Dana girls, who set the bags on the landing of the stairway.

"How do you do? I am Nat Kaner," the visitor introduced himself. "Valet to Mr. Warrington. I learned of Mrs. Zerbe's demise and came to talk to you about her."

Jean and Louise glanced quickly at each other, for they well remembered their uncle's recent remarks concerning the man.

"Won't you come in, Mr. Kaner?" invited Mrs. Borden politely. "I'll tell you anything I can."

It seemed to Louise and Jean that the servant was acting a part. Although he expressed deep sorrow at Mrs. Zerbe's death his words held no sincerity. He began at once to ask questions about the old lady's property and whether or not she made any deathbed statement.

"She didn't by chance mention a secret which concerned Mr. Warrington?" he inquired.

"No, she didn't," Mrs. Borden replied in annoyance.

"I merely ask this in the interest of my employer," Mr. Kaner said smoothly. "Now regarding Mrs. Zerbe's personal belongings. Of course Mr. Warrington is the person to receive them. I'll be glad to deliver them for you."

"These girls, Louise and Jean Dana," she said, nodding toward the two on the landing, "already have promised to do so," said Mrs. Borden, beginning to distrust the stranger. "The bags are ready to go now."

Nat Kaner's gaze came to rest upon the luggage which stood on the stairway landing.

"I could take these and save you girls a trip to the estate," he said persuasively to the Danas.

"Thank you," replied Louise dryly, "we don't mind going to a little trouble."

Presently, when his arguments were of no avail, the man took his leave; or at least Mrs. Borden and the girls assumed that he had left the grounds. However, after they had gone upstairs again Louise thought she heard a sound in the lower part of the house.

Going quickly to the stairway she gave an exclamation of impatience. Nat Kaner had slipped into the dwelling and was rummaging through Mrs. Zerbe's luggage.

"What are you doing?" Louise cried angrily, starting down the stairs.

"Just looking," the red-haired man retorted coolly. "Well, so long."

Quickly he went out the front door, slamming it behind him. The girls examined the bags but could discover nothing missing.

"I don't believe he found what he was after," declared Louise in relief. "He probably expected to locate papers of some sort."

"The fellow ought to be arrested!" Mrs. Borden exclaimed indignantly. "The very idea, walking boldly into a person's house!"

Louise and Jean carried the luggage to their home, intending to take it with them when they should return to Starhurst School. Since they had accepted an invitation to a dance that evening the girls spent the balance of the late afternoon preparing for it.

Returning home from the gay festivities at midnight, Jean was startled to observe a shadowy figure slinking around the corner of the Dana house. Instantly she became convinced that the person was Nat Kaner. Louise agreed with her sister. Boldly they called the man by name. While they could hear a movement among the bushes, he did not reply to them. The girls' escorts looked around but could find no one.

"That snooping fellow probably knows we have Mrs. Zerbe's luggage and means to gain possession of it," Jean whispered to her sister as the girls entered the house. "What if he should prowl around here all night?"

"We should call the police."

Going upstairs, the girls awakened their uncle and told their story. He telephoned to Headquarters, explaining the situation. While waiting for the officers to arrive Captain Dana and his nieces searched the grounds, but the mysterious prowler had gone. During the remainder of the night a policeman remained on guard but there was no further disturbance.

The next morning Louise and Jean went to see some of their friends who were also home for the holidays. Their aunt and uncle, deciding to pay a call in the next town, spoke seriously to Cora Appel before leaving. The maid was warned to maintain a close watch of the premises. Shortly before twelve the Dana girls returned to find no one at home and doors and windows unlocked.

"Where is Cora?" Louise asked in dismay. "She shouldn't have gone off and left the place."

"I hope nothing has been taken!" cried Jean, worried.

Quickly the girls ran to their room to make certain Mrs. Zerbe's luggage was safe. They were greatly relieved to see three bags standing by the bed where they had been left. However, Jean thought suddenly that the leather on them looked different. As she bent to examine the suitcases more closely, she found them to be cheap and quite unlike what the deceased woman had owned.

"Louise!" she exclaimed in a tense voice, "we've been tricked! These bags aren't the ones we brought from Mrs. Borden's place!"

CHAPTER IX

THE STOLEN LUGGAGE

As the two girls examined the substituted bags, they discovered them to be stuffed with old rags and a few stones to give them weight.

"Nat Kaner must have stolen Mrs. Zerbe's luggage," Louise declared indignantly. "I suppose he is miles away from Oak Falls by now."

"Probably," agreed Jean gloomily. "Yet there's a possibility that the thief may have been that stranger Mrs. Borden told us about— the man who kept bothering Mrs. Zerbe."

"Not very likely. Let's talk with Mrs. Borden before we leave Oak Falls. The thing for us to do now is to try to locate Nat Kaner if he's still in town."

"I don't see how the house was entered."

"It wouldn't be very difficult for a person to get in with no one at home," replied Louise. "One simply can't rely on Applecore to carry out instructions."

After revealing the loss to their aunt and uncle when they returned, the Dana girls hastened to the railroad station to inquire if anyone answering Kaner's description had been

75

seen there. The ticket agent replied in the negative, at the same time saying he had not observed anyone carrying bags resembling those stolen. Discouraged, the girls called at several bus stations, then went to Mrs. Borden's home to report to her what had occurred.

"Now don't feel bad about it," the woman said kindly. "It wasn't your fault, and I can't see that any great harm has been done. Mrs. Zerbe's clothing was of no real value."

"Nevertheless, we'll do everything we can to recover the property," Jean promised, not revealing that she thought there might be a very unhappy outcome to the episode. "We plan to run down every possible clue. Can you tell us more about that stranger who came to see Mrs. Zerbe?" she asked.

"There isn't much to tell. He was about twenty-five or twenty-six years of age, I'd say. Black eyes and curly hair, and a conceited air about him."

"Why, that sounds like a description of Abe Mantel!" Louise exclaimed. "Don't you think so, Jean?"

"It does a little. But what would he be doing in Oak Falls?"

"He's trying to find out everything he can concerning Mr. Warrington's business affairs. Probably he thought he could induce Mrs. Zerbe to talk about them."

"The man hasn't been back since the funeral?'' Jean asked Mrs. Borden thoughtfully.

"I've not seen him,'' was the woman's reply.

After discussing every angle of the strange case, Louise and Jean said good-bye to Mrs. Borden and hastened home. They barely had enough time to pack their own belongings and catch the train for Penfield. Their aunt accompanied them to the station.

"While we're gone will you watch for Nat Kaner?'' Jean requested her relative as she kissed her good-bye. "He may be still somewhere around Oak Falls.''

"I certainly shall,'' promised Miss Dana. "I've never heard of anything more brazen than stealing luggage from a house in broad daylight.''

The train came in and the girls swung aboard. As they took seats Lettie Briggs sauntered down the aisle, pausing before them. She wore a new fur coat and deliberately assumed all kinds of poses so that they would not fail to notice how well it fitted her.

"Santa Claus must have visited you early this year,'' remarked Louise, smiling. "What sort of fur is it—dyed muskrat?''

"Dyed muskrat!'' Lettie retorted in an injured tone. "Too bad you can't tell genuine sable when you see it.''

"Whatever it is, it's very pretty,'' said Jean evenly. "I hope it wears well. It seems to be shedding a bit.''

"All fur coats do that when they are new," Lettie replied, turning away angrily.

Arriving at Penfield, the Dana girls learned there was trouble with the heating plant at Starhurst School and they would have two hours of freedom before they would have to report. They decided to make use of the time by visiting the Warrington estate at once, since they considered it their duty to report the theft of Mrs. Zerbe's luggage.

Reaching the grounds, Louise and Jean found the gate locked and Bert Badger nowhere in evidence. They called his name and rang the bell but he did not appear. As they were about to turn away, the man emerged from the gatehouse.

"Sorry to have kept you waiting," he said in an agitated voice. "We've had a pretty upsetting time of it here today."

"Is anything wrong?" inquired Louise quickly.

"Oh, no—that is, I can't tell you," the guard muttered. "In fact, I don't know whether or not I ought to let you in."

"We've come on a very important mission," Louise said firmly. "We can't leave without delivering a certain message."

"Well, I guess it will be all right," Badger decided, reluctantly swinging open the heavy gate.

Louise and Jean walked directly to the mansion and rang the doorbell. Again they were compelled to wait. The butler who finally admitted them seemed to be in a state of excitement which he vainly endeavored to hide.

"You came to see Miss Evangeline?" he questioned the girls as they stepped into the hallway.

"Yes," replied Jean, "or Mr. Warrington."

"You cannot see him," the butler declared firmly. "I'll take you upstairs to Miss Evangeline."

As they mounted the circular stairway, the Dana girls became aware of a low murmur of voices from the direction of the living room. It struck them that they had been hurried away lest the conversation reach their ears. Clearly something was wrong in the Warrington household.

"Will you wait here, please?" the butler requested, leading the way into a tiny sitting room on the second floor. "I will tell Miss Evangeline you are calling."

The door closed behind the servant but the latch did not snap. Slowly it swung partly open. Jean and Louise distinctly heard the sound of weeping from Miss Warrington's bedroom.

"What *do* you suppose has happened?" the younger girl whispered in bewilderment.

The butler returned before Louise had an opportunity to express an opinion, indicating that the girls might see the young woman. Miss

Warrington sat with her back to the door.
Hastily she powdered her face to cover the tear
stains, then arose to greet the callers.

The girls scarcely knew how to proceed. Ignoring the young woman's distress, they spoke
of the telegram which had been sent to Mr.
Warrington announcing Mrs. Zerbe's death.

"Oh, my father never received it!" Miss
Warrington exclaimed. "Oh, poor Mrs. Zerbe.
When did she die?"

Louise explained by asking again:

"Then your father never learned of Mrs.
Zerbe's death?"

As Miss Warrington shook her head the
Danas concluded that probably Nat Kaner had
intercepted their wire.

"Father would have attended the funeral if it
had been possible. He thought the world of
Mrs. Zerbe."

"And she had a deep affection for him. May
we speak with your father, please? Jean and I
have an important matter to discuss with him."

"I can't grant you your request, I'm afraid.
I truly wish I could."

"No doubt your father is very busy," Jean
acknowledged. "Still, there is something we
learned which we think he should know."

"Can you tell it to me instead?"

Jean shook her head. "It concerns a secret
matter. However, we have two reasons for
coming here today. We were asked to deliver

Mrs. Zerbe's personal belongings to your father. Unfortunately the bags were stolen from us."

"Oh," murmured Miss Warrington in surprise. "Well, I shall tell Father when I see him."

Jean and Louise were unable to understand the young woman's reluctance to permit them to talk with the man. As they turned to leave a light tap was heard on the door.

"Come in," invited Miss Warrington.

Mr. McCarter, the detective whom the Dana girls previously had met, stepped into the room. He looked in surprise at the callers.

"Oh, I'm sorry," he apologized. "I didn't know you had visitors, Miss Warrington."

"We were just leaving," replied Louise, moving toward the door.

"Just a minute, please," the detective requested. "Since you are here I should like to ask a question or two. You don't mind?"

"Is it about the missing dog?" Jean inquired with a shade of impatience.

"No," smiled the detective, "I merely wish to ask about your acquaintance with a Mrs. Zerbe. When did you first meet her?"

"About a week or ten days ago," returned Louise. "We chanced upon her while we were on our way home from a hike."

"I understand Mrs. Zerbe was inclined to be talkative. Did she mention anything about Mr. Warrington's affairs?"

"She said that he was a very kind, generous employer," replied Louise.

"And that he gave her a liberal pension," added Jean.

"I scarcely referred to that," said the detective, frowning. "Did Mrs. Zerbe tell you anything about her life here?"

"Only that she and her husband had lived for many years at the gatehouse," responded Louise, surprised at the question.

"Did she mention any friends of hers?"

"We talked with her only a few minutes. She spoke of no one who was a personal acquaintance of hers."

"She expressed no dislike for Mr. Warrington, no resentment at having been sent away by him?"

"Quite the contrary. She seemed to feel that he had treated her fairly in every way. But why are you asking us all these questions?"

"Oh, merely to get the record straight," the detective answered vaguely. "Mrs. Zerbe had a long and interesting association with Mr. Warrington. She lived here a long while."

"It's very obvious a special investigation is being conducted," declared Jean with spirit. "My sister and I don't feel like telling you anything more until we have an idea why we are being questioned."

"You have a right to know the truth. I will

tell you what has happened," spoke up Miss Warrington unexpectedly.

"Do you feel such a policy would be wise?" interposed Mr. McCarter hastily. "We must keep the news out of the papers, you know."

"Jean and I never betray a confidence," said Louise quietly.

The girls waited, fearful that Miss Warrington, influenced by the detective, might change her mind. However, the young woman seemed to feel that she could trust the Danas for she said in a low tone vibrant with emotion:

"I did not mean to be rude a moment ago in refusing you an audience with my father. The truth is, he has disappeared!"

CHAPTER X

A Deceiving Signature

Before Louise and Jean had an opportunity to make further inquiries, Mr. Hinkley, the lawyer, entered the room.

"Miss Warrington, you are wanted on the telephone in the study," he said urgently. "The lodgekeeper Badger wants to speak to you. He says he has important information about your father, but refuses to talk with anyone except you."

"I'll take the call," the young woman said eagerly, arising from her chair.

Excusing herself, she went to a near-by room where she could speak without being overheard.

"Is it thought that Mr. Warrington has been kidnaped?" Louise asked, turning to the detective.

"So far we have no definite clue. Mr. Warrington started for his office the other day and has not been seen since."

"Would he have a reason for wishing to disappear?" asked Jean significantly.

The detective gave her a shrewd glance. "Couldn't say," he answered dryly. "I'm here to make a complete investigation, and until I do, I have no opinion to give out."

84

"Are you working in Mr. Warrington's interests?" inquired Louise.

"I am. His daughter has asked me to undertake the case," the man replied formally.

At that moment the young woman returned, her agitation disclosing that she had gained important information.

"The gatekeeper has found a note!" she exclaimed, directing her remarks to the detective. "It was left in a tree not far from the entrance."

"A ransom demand?"

"I think so. Badger was so excited he didn't speak plainly. The note said that Father would return home in four days if we would meet certain demands."

"How much did the writer want?"

"I couldn't understand Badger. He did say the note was signed 'Collar-Button Cad.'"

"It sounds like a hoax to me," spoke up Mr. Hinkley decisively.

"Oh, it may not be," declared Miss Warrington, sinking into the nearest chair. "I feel certain Father never would have gone away without letting me know. I believe he is being detained against his will."

As the distressed young woman began to weep, Jean went to her side and tried to comfort her.

"We'll have a look at that note," announced the detective grimly, ringing for a servant, whom he asked to bring the message from the gatehouse.

While they waited, Louise and Jean drew to one side where they consulted in whispers. The discovery of the note suggested two possibilities to them; Abe Mantel might have planted it in the tree as a hoax, or the message could have been composed by the valet, Nat Kaner.

"Wouldn't the latter be likely to sign himself 'Collar Button Cad'?" reasoned Jean. "I associate the signature with his duties as valet. He's the sort of individual who would write a threatening message. Knowing so much about Mr. Warrington's business affairs he might use the knowledge to benefit himself."

Soon the servant returned with a scrap of soiled yellow paper. Mr. McCarter read the note, which stated that Mr. Warrington would be returned home unharmed providing certain ransom demands were met promptly. What the demands consisted of was not mentioned, although the writer promised a more definite communication within a few days.

"In my opinion, this is someone's idea of a joke," the detective declared as he finished reading the message and offered it to Miss Warrington. "Bert Badger may have composed it, hoping to ingratiate himself with you."

"This doesn't look like the man's handwriting," protested Miss Warrington as she studied the message.

Jean and Louise hoped they would be given an opportunity to examine the note carefully, but the young woman folded it and locked it in a drawer.

"I shall be guided by your judgment, Mr. McCarter," she said in a low tone. "When the demands are made I shall be in favor of meeting them. Father means everything to me."

Tears glistened in her eyes.

"We don't want to do anything rash," Mr. McCarter argued. "You let me handle this."

"By the way," interposed Louise unexpectedly, turning to the young woman, "whatever became of your father's valet, Nat Kaner?"

Miss Warrington regarded the Dana girl with startled eyes.

"Why, that is an angle we haven't considered! My father discharged the man several weeks ago. I haven't seen him since."

Given an opening, Louise and Jean proceeded to put forth a few of the facts in their possession, mentioning Kaner's unsavory reputation in shipping circles and his mysterious visit to Oak Falls. While refraining from making a direct accusation against the man, they suggested that he might have been the person who signed the note.

"Maybe you have a clue at that!" exclaimed McCarter in honest admiration. "At least it is worth tracing down. Kaner may have held a grudge against Mr. Warrington. I'll get in touch with the police and have them bring the man in for questioning.''

''There must be no publicity,'' the missing man's daughter warned the detective. ''You know how the newspapers seize upon any item and elaborate upon it beyond recognition.''

''The whole affair will be kept quiet,'' the man promised. ''That is, if every person in this room takes a vow of secrecy.''

''Mr. Warrington's interests are mine also,'' said Mr. Hinkley stiffly.

''Jean and I never will divulge the information,'' added Louise quickly, speaking for her sister as well.

The girls talked a little longer with Miss Warrington. Then as the two hours of grace was nearly up, they returned to Starhurst School. They were somewhat amused to find a group of students clustered about Lettie Briggs admiring her new fur coat, which she was saying was genuine sable. The Dana girls did not join them, but went at once to their suite.

Classes began as usual the following morning. Louise and Jean were kept busy with their studies but again and again they thought of Mr. Warrington's strange disappearance. The afternoon brought a telegram from their Aunt Harriet which stirred their interest in the case to fever pitch.

The message revealed that following their departure from Oak Falls, Miss Dana had conversed with the owner of a cigar and newspaper stand. He told her that a red-haired fellow answering Nat Kaner's description had bought cigarettes from him the previous day, and that the three leather bags which resembled those stolen from the Dana home had been in his possession at the time.

"This tends to confirm our original theory!" Jean cried as she excitedly turned the message over to her sister.

"I wish Aunt Harriet had given us additional details," Louise said, frowning as she read the brief communication. "She didn't even mention the name of the man who operates the stand."

"Why not telephone to her?" proposed Jean impulsively.

"Well—" Louise debated. "You know how it is, using the dormitory phones. Someone always dashes in when I'm in the midst of a conversation, and I cannot speak freely."

"Especially Lettie. It's an old trick of hers to do that," added Jean.

"We might go to Penfield after classes," Louise went on thoughtfully. "Then we can phone in peace."

"Yes, let's," agreed Jean. "Nobody will overhear our conversation there. We can call Aunt Harriet from one of the drugstores."

The Dana girls finished their last class for the day at three o'clock. In their haste to catch a bus into town they did not notice that Ina Mason was watching their departure with particular interest.

"Let's try Reiley's drugstore," Louise proposed as the sisters alighted in Penfield. "The place usually is deserted at this hour."

The telephone booths were located at the rear of the store. As Jean started to enter one of the enclosures she suddenly grabbed Louise's arm.

"Look who is inside that booth!" she whispered. "Abe Mantel!"

The older girl took one glance, then pushed her sister into the open compartment adjoining. Neither one had been noticed by the man.

"Hello!" they heard the reporter say in a clear voice. "Give me the editor! Yeah, I've got a tip on a big story! Somebody important around here has skipped out!"

Deeply interested, Jean and Louise stood perfectly still. Could he be talking about Mr. Warrington? Had the news of the man's disappearance leaked out?

CHAPTER XI

AN EXCITING NIGHT

"LISTEN, Chief," Abe Mantel called into the telephone. "I have a big scoop for you! Richard Warrington has skipped out! Yes, that's right. He's afraid to face the investigation so he decided to vanish. Haven't been able to get all the facts yet, but you can run this much at least."

"All the facts," Jean murmured indignantly. "He's making up every bit of that. Even Miss Warrington doesn't know what has become of her father."

"The story must never be printed," Louise declared. "We've got to do something about it."

"Let's try to reason with Abe Mantel and get him to retract that statement."

Slipping out of the telephone booth, the girls waited until the reporter had finished his conversation. As he emerged he nodded carelessly to them, then started away.

"Oh, just a minute, Mr. Mantel," Jean said quickly. "We'd like to ask you something."

"I'm in a big hurry," the man returned, scowling. "You'll have to talk fast."

"We couldn't help overhearing your conversation," Louise began earnestly. "We ask you not to publish that story about Mr. Warrington."

"Why not?"

"Because it isn't true as you very well know. You are only guessing."

"Perhaps I am, but it's a shrewd guess."

"You'll cause the Warrington family untold embarrassment if you print the story," Jean argued. "Call the editor and tell him that you cannot confirm your facts!"

"And lose a promotion?" the reporter queried jeeringly. "Like fun I will."

He started to move on, only to have Jean catch his arm.

"You must listen," she pleaded. "You don't realize what you are doing."

"Let me go!" the reporter said angrily.

He gave the girl a push which shoved her against a group of chairs. One of them toppled over, making such a disturbance it brought the proprietor to the scene.

"What's going on here?" the man demanded irritably.

Abe Mantel did not wait to explain. Jamming down his hat over his eyes, he rushed past the Dana girls and dashed out the front door.

"I'm sorry," Jean apologized, stooping to right the chair. "We were only trying to make that man listen to reason."

Deeply embarrassed, the two girls hurried to
the street. By that time the reporter had disappeared.

"The story will be published," Louise said
bitterly. "Probably Miss Warrington will
blame us, thinking we did not keep our promise
of secrecy."

"I think we should go out to the estate and
tell her everything. Mr. McCarter may be able
to do something to prevent the printing of the
story."

"There's a chance it can be killed if we act
quickly," agreed Louise. "Come along. We
haven't a minute to lose."

At the Warrington home Bert Badger admitted the girls without question for by this time
he knew they were welcome callers. Learning
that Mr. McCarter was not at the mansion,
Louise and Jean asked to see Evangeline and
were shown into her presence. Tersely they related to her what they had overheard in the telephone booth, while she listened intently.

"Mr. McCarter has gone away for the day,"
declared Miss Warrington in great agitation.
"He is tracing down a clue which he considers
very important."

The Danas were disappointed.

"Then we can't depend upon him to help us,"
said Louise quickly. "Anything that is to be
done must be done at once."

"Would it do any good if I were to go to the

editor and plead with him not to run the story?" asked Miss Warrington.

"It might," said Jean. "At least it would be worth trying."

"Will you and Louise go with me?"

"Yes, of course."

The young woman called for a coupe, which was brought to the door by a colored chauffeur. Ten minutes later the party reached the offices of the Penfield *Post*. After a long wait the three were escorted into the presence of the editor.

"Well?" he asked with an unpleasant inflection in his voice.

"I think you know who I am and why I am here," said Miss Warrington with quiet dignity. "The story which your reporter, Mr. Mantel, telephoned in a few minutes ago about my father is without truth. I came to ask you please not to print it."

"If your father didn't skip out to avoid a government investigation, then where is he?" demanded the editor.

"I cannot tell you."

"Very well, if you'll not cooperate with us, don't expect us to do you any favors. Sorry, but we'll run the facts as we have them."

"That's exactly the point I'm trying to stress," Miss Warrington argued. "The story is untrue and would be most damaging to my father's reputation if it were printed. Why not treat us fairly?"

Both Jean and Louise sought to influence the editor, but without success. At length he arose, a gesture signifying that the interview was terminated. Disheartened, the three girls left the man's office.

At exactly the moment when the Danas were entering Miss Warrington's car, Lettie and Ina happened to be coming down the street. They paused to stare in amazement.

"It beats all how those girls manage to hobnob with society folks," grumbled Ina Mason enviously.

"I wonder what they've been doing in the newspaper office?" speculated Lettie. "I'll bet it had something to do with a story they're afraid may be printed!"

As the coupe drove away the two girls started walking down the street. At the entrance to the Penfield *Post* they met Abe Mantel who was leaving the building.

"Hello there, Mr. Mantel," said Lettie boldly. "Don't you remember me?"

"Oh, hello," he greeted the girl carelessly. "What do you know today?"

"Nothing about the Warrington case, I'm afraid," she replied.

"I'm one jump ahead of you then," he laughed in a boastful way. "We're coming out with a big scoop—all about how the big man skipped to avoid an investigation."

"Won't I enjoy reading that!" chuckled Lettie. "I'll order fifty copies so I can send them to all of the Dana girls' friends!"

Unaware that the story of Mr. Warrington's disappearance already was being circulated, Jean and Louise rode back to Starhurst School in Evangeline's car.

"I dread staying at home since Father has disappeared," the young woman remarked. "I wish you girls could spend the night with me."

"I don't suppose Mrs. Crandall would let us leave the school," Louise replied regretfully, "though she might consider it if you were to ask her."

"I'll be very glad to talk with her."

Upon being approached by the girls, and hearing the entire story, Mrs. Crandall hesitated at first, but later agreed that the Danas might spend the night at the estate. The Warringtons were a highly respected family in the community despite all the rumors directed against them. Then too, Evangeline's father often had made generous donations to Starhurst, so the headmistress decided it might be best to accede to the girl's wishes.

Lettie and her small group of friends did not take these facts into consideration when they learned of the special privilege granted to Louise and Jean. They went about telling everyone that favoritism was being shown for no reason at all.

Dinner at the Warrington mansion was a

lengthy meal which the Danas enjoyed thoroughly. However, they could not fail to notice their hostess's increasing uneasiness as the evening wore on. At nine o'clock Bert Badger, coming to the house, asked to see the visitors.

"I want to ask a big favor of you," he said soberly as they appeared. "Would you be willing to spend the night at the gatehouse?"

"Why should we do that?" Louise queried in astonishment.

"I want to get away for the evening. I have a hunch I may know something about Mr. Warrington's disappearance."

"What is your information, Badger?" inquired Miss Warrington who had stepped to the door.

"I can't tell anyone about it, Miss Evangeline. The errand will have to be kept a secret."

"You want the night off to investigate?"

"Yes, Miss. I thought if someone were to take my place at the gatehouse you wouldn't have any objections. It isn't likely anyone will come to be let in this late at night, but the gate ought to be guarded."

"We'll be glad to stay there," offered Jean instantly. "That is, if Miss Warrington has no objection."

"I have none, though I dread remaining alone in the mansion with only the servants. I might spend the night at the gatehouse myself."

"Oh, please do," Louise declared heartily.

"Three guards are always better than two!"

As Badger wished to leave at once the three girls assembled a few belongings and went to the gatehouse. The tiny dwelling was plainly, though comfortably, furnished.

"I'd suggest that you retire early," Jean advised Evangeline. "Louise and I will take turns keeping watch throughout the night."

"I'd like to do my share."

"You are very tired and you need rest and sleep. Louise and I can afford to do without them better than you can."

After Miss Warrington had followed their suggestion and retired, the two Dana girls took turns listening for callers. Hour after hour dragged by, but no one sought admittance nor attempted to scale the wall.

"This is a more exasperating task than I had anticipated," Jean declared shortly after midnight as she prepared to relieve her sister at her post. "Has anything happened during the past hour?"

"Nothing. I've been searching about in the gatehouse for lack of something else to do. I can't figure out what Mr. Warrington's mysterious secret might be."

"Better get some sleep," advised Jean. "You'll be tired out tomorrow if you don't."

Louise started to leave, only to pause and listen attentively.

"What was that?" she asked in a whisper.

"It sounds like someone digging in the basement."

The two girls huddled together, attempting to identify the strange noise which seemed to come from beneath the floor.

"It does sound like someone digging and throwing dirt around," Jean said uneasily. "Shall we find out what it is?"

Summoning their courage, the two sisters tiptoed to the cellar doorway and peered into the dark cavern below them.

CHAPTER XII

BADGER'S ADVENTURE

"EVERYTHING seems to be all right," Louise
said uncertainly. "I only wish we had brought
our flashlight."

Without a means of illuminating the cellar,
the girls hesitated to venture alone into the darkness. They stood at the head of the stairs, listening a few minutes.

"It must have been a rat," Jean declared at
last. "Or possibly Sally has come home."

The Dana girls did not frighten Evangeline
by telling her of the disturbance. However,
they both were uneasy and decided to keep watch
together during the remaining hours of the
night.

Time dragged slowly, but dawn came at last,
streaking the eastern horizon with red and violet
rays. Yawning, Jean walked to the window of
the gatehouse.

"Bert Badger should be coming back soon,"
she remarked, "unless something has happened
to him. Where in the world do you suppose he
went and what clue did he have?"

"I haven't the faintest idea. I don't see how

he could have obtained any clue as to Mr. Warrington's disappearance. It's my guess that was only an excuse for getting away. He had something else in mind to do.''

"Do you know, Louise, it struck me that his mysterious errand might have had to do with Abe Mantel.''

"What makes you think that?''

"Nothing in particular, except that last evening when we arrived I chanced to mention to Badger what had happened at the newspaper office. He was furious and said he would like to get even with Abe Mantel for playing such a mean trick.''

"Still that doesn't prove anything. A person often makes idle threats without meaning them,'' Louise replied wisely.

"I know,'' admitted Jean, "but Badger acted as if he were thinking over the matter——''

Breaking off rather abruptly, she raised the window sash. A small folded sheet of paper fluttered to the floor at her feet.

"What is that?'' questioned Louise, hurrying across the room.

"I just this moment noticed it. Someone must have left it on the window sill during the night!''

Stooping, Jean picked up the paper and spread it on the table so that they could read the message. In a bold scrawl appeared a few penciled words.

*"Bert Badger: Either mind your own
affairs or take the consequence! A hint to
the wise is sufficient!"*

"Well, did you ever!" murmured Jean in astonishment. "Who could have left this warning?"

"No one entered through the gate last night,
but someone must have prowled about the
grounds."

"I wish now that we had investigated the cellar when we heard that noise."

"I don't," said Louise firmly. "It would
have been a rash thing since we had no light and
didn't even know what the place looks like."

"It's queer Badger should be threatened,"
Jean declared thoughtfully as she refolded the
message. "I wonder if he too has some deep
secret he is hiding?"

"Listen!" Louise warned, grasping her sister's hand. "Someone is trying to get in the
gate."

Hurrying outside, the girls smiled in relief
for it was none other than Bert Badger. His
clothing was rumpled and his hands were covered with grease, but he greeted them with an
expansive smile.

"Oh, we're glad to see you back safe," Jean
said quickly. "Did you have a successful night
in your investigation?" she asked.

"Quite an adventure," he chuckled. "Yes, a

highly successful one, but I can't tell you about
it. How did you get along here?"

"All right," answered Louise, studying the
gatekeeper curiously. "However, we thought
we heard someone in the cellar. Just a few minutes ago we found this note on the window ledge,
addressed to you."

Badger took the paper, scanning the message
at a glance. To the amazement of the Dana girls
he seemed not in the least disturbed by its contents. Thrusting the note carelessly into his
pocket he said:

"I'll take over my duties now. Thank you for
looking after things. You better go to the house
and try to get some sleep."

"Aren't you worried about the warning?"
Jean asked him curiously.

"It takes more than a warning to bother me,"
the man chuckled. "Don't you do any worrying
about Bert Badger! He knows how to take care
of himself."

The girls longed to ask the watchman where
he had been and why his clothing was so dirty,
but they knew from his secretive manner that he
would not tell them. They suspected too that he
had a very good idea as to who had written the
anonymous note, but that he was not telling this
either.

Reentering the gatehouse, Louise and Jean
awakened Evangeline. The three returned to
the big house. Worn out from their long vigil,

the Dana girls slept until after nine o'clock. At that time a maid brought them breakfast on trays together with an early morning edition of the Penfield *Post*.

"Oh, I'm afraid to look at it," Jean declared, reaching to unfold the newssheet. "The Warrington story will be spread across the front page, I know."

"I feel sorry for Evangeline," added Louise. "But there was nothing we could do to stop Abe Mantel's story."

As Jean opened the paper a blank expression came over her face. There were no glaring headlines nor photographs of any member of the Warrington family. In fact, the front page contained no important story; only an assortment of small items, making an uninteresting front page.

"This is funny," she murmured, quickly glancing through the rest of the paper. "Louise, the Warrington story wasn't printed! And the whole sheet is only about half the usual size."

"Something must have happened at the plant so the men couldn't get out the regular edition," declared Louise gleefully. "See, this isn't their usual style of make-up. They've set it up in a different type."

Dressing hurriedly, the girls went to Evangeline's room. The young woman already had seen the morning paper and was in a cheerful mood, because she too had expected that the story would be published.

"Isn't it wonderful?" cried Jean.

"I am sure the editor meant to print the article," Miss Warrington said speculatively. "I wonder what could have happened to stop him from doing so?"

That afternoon the *Evening Journal,* a rival newspaper, published an answer to the girls' questions. The front page carried a box story stating that vandals had broken into the offices of the tabloid newssheet; destroyed type and forms; and caused great inconvenience in the printing of the early edition.

"So that is why the story about Father failed to appear!" exclaimed Evangeline as she read the item. "The forms must have been wrecked just about the time the paper was to go to press. How very fortunate for me that it happened!"

"Yes," said Jean, glancing at her sister. "It seems as if someone did it to save you, Miss Warrington."

Although the Dana girls did not say so, they wondered if Bert Badger might not be the person best able to explain the mysterious occurrence. The more they thought about it the more certain they became that this was the truth.

While they were examining the tabloid newspaper again, laughing over its ridiculous appearance, a servant showed Mr. McCarter into the living room. The detective looked as if he too had been up half the previous night, for his eyes were bloodshot and he walked with a weary step.

"Good afternoon, Miss Warrington," he said, sinking into the nearest chair and nodding to the Danas. "I regret that I have nothing encouraging to report."

"You've found no trace of Father?"

"Not a clue, although I've been on the job constantly during the past twenty-four hours. No luck in running down that fellow Nat Kaner, either. He seems to have disappeared into thin air," the detective said wearily.

"I'm growing more frightened and worried every hour," confessed Miss Warrington. "Don't you think we should call in Federal agents?"

"That would not be my advice," replied Mr. McCarter. "Give me another day and I think I can produce results."

"We've been fortunate in one respect at least," the young woman admitted. "The tabloid paper did not run an untrue story about Father's disappearance."

As the detective had not heard any details of the affair, he listened attentively when Louise and Jean offered a complete account of the experience with the newspaper editor. They likewise mentioned their belief that faithful Bert Badger might have been the person responsible for the destruction of the forms.

"A very clever piece of deduction," praised the man. "I shouldn't be surprised if you've hit the nail exactly on the head. Perhaps it will be just as well if we don't ask the lodge-keeper too many questions, eh?"

The Danas liked Mr. McCarter and felt that he was doing everything in his power to solve the mystery of Mr. Warrington's disappearance. They wondered if they should tell him of the note which Mrs. Zerbe had received from her employer mentioning a mysterious secret at the gatehouse. They decided for the present to withhold this information.

A telephone bell rang. Presently a servant came to report that Mr. McCarter was wanted on the wire. After answering the call he returned to the living room looking somewhat troubled.

"I must leave at once," he said to the girls. "When I get back we'll delve deeper into this whole matter."

Since the detective's call seemed to depress Evangeline, the Danas attempted to distract the young woman's mind from thinking of her troubles. Louise and Jean chatted about many subjects, introducing the topic of ancestry as one of them. Miss Warrington talked enthusiastically of her family, mentioning that her grandfather had made a special study of genealogy which had proven them to be descendants of a famous old English family.

"I'll show you the book that records it," she stated proudly.

Before the volume could be brought, another caller arrived. The newcomer proved to be an old man who appeared to be at least ninety years of age, although he still walked spryly with the aid of a cane. Evangeline, greeting him enthusiastically, told the Danas that he was Doctor Morgan, a physician, who during his former active practice had attended her family.

"Doctor Morgan knows all the Warrington secrets," the young woman said lightly. "He took care of my grandmother at the time Father was born. He has been giving us pills and advice ever since," she added with a smile.

"Advice which usually is disregarded," the elderly physician replied with a kindly smile. "Yes, I know all the Warrington secrets—sometimes I wish I didn't."

"Why, Doctor Morgan!" exclaimed Evangeline, surprised by his tone. "We haven't any skeletons in our closet, have we?"

"I was only joking," the doctor replied hastily. "Now don't fret your pretty head, Eve. Tell me, where is your father? I came to say good-bye to him. In a few days I'm leaving for the South to spend the winter."

Miss Warrington stared at the elderly man in astonishment. "Then you don't know?" she murmured.

"Know what, Eve?"

"That Father is missing. He disappeared under very strange circumstances."

Shocked by the news, Doctor Morgan asked for all the details of the case. During its recital Louise chanced to mention the death of Mrs. Zerbe and her last request. The physician seemed deeply impressed by the added information.

"So Mrs. Zerbe has passed on," he said sadly. "Poor old lady! Her life was an unhappy one after her husband's death but no one could lighten her burden."

"Did you know her well?" Jean questioned the man, watching him closely.

"Only slightly," replied the doctor uneasily. With an effort he arose from his chair. "I must be going now," he said.

"I'll walk with you to your car," offered Evangeline, taking her friend's arm.

Doctor Morgan said no more about Mrs. Zerbe. When Louise tried to bring up the subject again he skillfully changed it.

"Do you know what I think?" she whispered to Jean as the others left the room. "I believe old Doctor Morgan was quite serious when he spoke of possessing the Warrington secrets!"

CHAPTER XIII

THE WALL PANEL

SUDDENLY the girls were startled to hear a loud yell from the direction of the gatehouse. As they rushed to the porch of the mansion, a crash came from the interior of the little building, as if a piece of furniture had been hurled against a wall.

"What has happened?" Jean exclaimed.

Leaving Evangeline to look after the aged physician, Louise and Jean ran toward the lodge to see what was wrong. Reaching the doorway they were horrified to see Bert Badger and Abe Mantel struggling on the floor. The reporter was getting much the worse of the battle for the gatekeeper was pummeling him hard and steadily. A chair had been broken and furniture was scattered about everywhere.

As the Dana girls wondered if they should interfere the fighting ceased. Abe Mantel was brought under control by his adversary.

"The sneak slipped in here and tried to beat me up!" panted the gatekeeper in explanation. "I guess this will teach him a lesson."

"You deserved a licking after the trick you played," retorted Abe Mantel, rubbing a rapidly swelling nose. "I'll get even with you yet!"

"Oh, no, you won't," said Badger, taking the reporter roughly by an arm. "You're marching out of here. If you know what's good for you, you'll not be back."

The intruder was shoved through the gate which was locked behind him. Muttering to himself, he went down the road. On the floor of the lodge the Danas found a key which fit the gate. Mantel must have dropped it!

"Oh, Mr. Badger," observed Jean suddenly in alarm, "you're hurt. Your face is bleeding!"

"It's nothing."

"You must go to the mansion and have the wounds bandaged. Doctor Morgan is there. He'll take care of you."

"I'll be all right," the man insisted, gingerly feeling of his cheek. "I oughtn't to leave this place."

"We'll remain on guard," promised Louise. "You better go to the house."

Reluctantly the man consented. In a few moments the girls saw him enter the mansion with Miss Warrington and Doctor Morgan.

"Let's find out how much damage has been done to the furniture here," suggested Louise as the door closed.

Entering the gatehouse they gazed about in consternation at the disordered living room.

Jean stooped to pick up a chair which had been overturned.

"Why do you suppose Abe Mantel made such a vicious attack upon Badger?" she asked thoughtfully.

"That's not hard to guess. He must have learned that Badger was the one who did so much damage at the newspaper office."

"I guess you're right. But how did he find out? My, wouldn't it be dreadful if the paper's accusations against Mr. Warrington should turn out to be true!"

"Eve would never recover from the shock," said Louise soberly. "Her father must be innocent. He seems like too fine a man to be a wrongdoer."

"I hope so, anyway. Isn't this place a wreck? Bert Badger was lucky he wasn't hurt badly," offered Jean.

A mirror had been broken and a lamp upset, while a picture dangled from the wall by only one cord. Reaching up to straighten it, Jean noticed a rectangular outline behind the huge frame.

"Louise, come here!" she called softly. "I think I've discovered something!"

Her sister peered at the marks, running her finger along the edges.

"It looks like a secret panel!" she declared in an excited voice. "Perhaps this is what was meant in the note to Mrs. Zerbe!"

Jean pressed on each square inch of the panel. After exploring for several minutes, her finger touched a spring. Suddenly a tiny section of wall slid back to reveal a hidden safe.

"Close the panel quickly!" warned Louise who stood near the window. "Bert Badger is coming back! Hurry!"

The girls barely had time to get the picture in place again when the gatekeeper entered the building, followed by a servant who had been sent to help straighten up the place.

"How are you feeling now?" Jean tried to ask calmly, hoping that the man would not notice her state of excitement.

"All right," Badger answered briefly. "Doctor Morgan did a good job of patching me up. A car is ready now to take you girls back to school."

The Danas gathered together their overnight apparel. Saying good-bye to Miss Warrington, they entered the waiting limousine.

"Do come and see me again," the young woman urged. "I am so lonesome, being here with only the servants."

"We certainly will if Mrs. Crandall can be induced to give us another leave of absence," Louise promised heartily.

The arrival of the big shiny car at Starhurst attracted considerable comment among the students. Lettie in particular was envious of the Dana girls, extremely jealous of the fact that

the beautiful heiress had singled them out for
her attention.

"Just you wait," she hinted to Ina Mason.
"The Warringtons won't think so highly of
them after they read tomorrow's newspaper."

Even before breakfast was served a flood of
tabloid newssheets ordered by Lettie descended
upon the dormitory. When Jean and Louise
came down to the front hall they observed that
nearly every girl in the room was there, absorbed in reading a front page story.

"What is this, free newspaper day around
here?" remarked Jean innocently enough.

Evelyn Starr came running up, one of the
sheets in her hand. She thrust it before the
eyes of the Dana girls.

"This is the lowest trick yet!" she exclaimed
angrily. "Read!"

The tabloid paper, the same one which had
sought to bring disgrace upon Evangeline Warrington, now bore a startling front page head-
line. Above a picture of Lettie Briggs in her
new fur coat was a caption reading:

"Valuable Sable Coat Stolen at Fashionable
School. Miss Briggs Accuses Dana Sisters."

"What!" cried Louise in disbelief. "She
dares to say we took her coat!"

"It's ridiculous!" added Jean. "Why, she
was wearing it day before yesterday. If she
thinks we had anything to do with her loss, why
didn't she speak to us about it?"

As the students were reading the account, Mrs. Crandall entered the hall, and her face was very stern.

"Young ladies," she said, speaking to the entire group, "by whom were these papers brought into the dormitory?"

"Fifty of them were thrown on the steps early this morning," replied one of the students. "I saw a newsboy leave them."

"Will each girl please bring her paper to this table?" requested the headmistress. "The copies will be burned."

"You can't destroy the entire edition," muttered Lettie rudely as she entered the hall. "I guess folks have a right to know the truth."

"Lettie, I wish to see you in my office at once," said Mrs. Crandall severely. "Louise and Jean, you come with me also."

The three girls followed the headmistress to her private room.

"Now we'll get to the bottom of this," she declared. "Lettie, is it true your fur coat has been lost?"

"It was stolen! The Dana girls took it from my closet!"

"Why did you not speak to me about the matter instead of making a public accusation?"

"Because I knew it would do no good," Lettie answered sullenly. "You always side with Louise and Jean."

"Usually for a very good reason. Perhaps

you don't realize it, Lettie, but your story has greatly damaged the reputation of the school as well as its students. I trust you are prepared to prove your charges.''

"It's up to the Dana girls to prove they didn't take the coat,'' Lettie replied, looking a trifle frightened.

"I believe we can do that,'' said Louise calmly. "And we can prove something else, too. Where did you buy your coat, Lettie?''

"My father bought it for me at Herman's in Oak Falls.''

"Just what I thought,'' nodded Louise, smiling, "and you say the coat is sable.''

"Certainly it is!''

"I happen to know that Herman's Store never has carried sable in stock. Your coat is nothing but dyed muskrat. If you wish me to prove it I'll telephone to the store by long distance and make sure.''

"No, don't do that,'' Lettie muttered, her eyes downcast.

"Then you admit that the coat was not made from sable skins?'' asked the Dana girl.

"Maybe it wasn't, but my father spent a lot of money for it. And you girls did take it out of my closet!''

"When was the coat removed?'' interposed Jean coolly.

"Night before last.''

The sisters now waited for Mrs. Crandall to speak.

"Lettie," the woman said sternly, "you have discredited yourself completely. Louise and Jean could not possibly have taken your coat night before last. They spent the entire evening at the Warrington estate. Now you must withdraw your charges at once or I shall take action against you!"

CHAPTER XIV

A Disguise

LETTIE had no choice but to tell the truth. She knew that Mrs. Crandall, thoroughly provoked by the unfavorable publicity, would expel her unless she did so.

"All right, I withdraw my charges," she muttered angrily. "I'll look for the coat again. I might find it."

"I am sure you will," returned the headmistress significantly. "Now explain about this picture which appears in the newspaper. You know it is against school rules."

"A reporter named Abe Mantel wanted to take it so I let him. I didn't suppose he would print everything I said. He made it sound a lot worse than I intended it to."

"You will have to retract your statement to the paper, Lettie, completely clearing Louise and Jean. I shall go with you to the newspaper office this afternoon. That will be all for the time being. Report to me as soon as you have found your coat."

Lettie vanished to her room where she spent an hour in a pretended search for the missing garment. Then she reappeared, acknowledging that she had located it tucked far back in the wardrobe closet.

"I guess Ina pushed it out of sight when I was gone," she explained glibly.

"Oh, no, I didn't," retorted her roommate. "You put the coat back there yourself. I saw you do it."

The newspaper retraction, together with Lettie's own admission of guilt, convinced all the students that the Danas had been quite blameless. They criticized the Briggs girl and expressed satisfaction upon learning that Mrs. Crandall had deprived her of every social privilege. In fact, they felt she should have had a more severe punishment.

During the next three days Louise and Jean devoted themselves diligently to their studies. Then the following morning they received a note from Miss Warrington, urging them to visit her as soon as they could.

"Oh, I hope Mrs. Crandall will let us go," said Jean eagerly.

Obtaining permission from the headmistress the girls telephoned to the mansion. In a little while the Warrington limousine called at the school for the Danas.

"I am so grateful that you came," Evangeline greeted the sisters cordially when they arrived at her home.

She was much thinner, they noticed, than when they had seen her before and her cheeks were pale. She must have worried a great deal indeed.

"Have you had any news from your father?" Jean asked when the door had closed behind them.

Evangeline sorrowfully shook her head. "Not a word. Mr. McCarter is having no luck in his search for him. I suppose you know what everyone is saying."

"That your father slipped away to avoid an investigation of his finances?" Louise supplied. "Yes, we've heard the rumors but we place no stock in them," she added quickly.

"You've both been such good friends," the young woman said, deeply moved. "Somehow you've given me courage. But it is so hard to wait for word of Father. If only I could do something myself!"

"I know how you feel," Jean nodded sympathetically.

She sank into a chair, absently picking up a newspaper lying there. It was the Calumet *Post,* published in a small city many miles away. Curiously Jean turned the pages, noticing that an advertisement in the lost and found column had been circled with a pencil.

"Oh, I intended to show that to you!" exclaimed Evangeline. "Someone sent me the paper with it marked as you see."

The item, confined to two lines, gave the information that a Great Dane had been found and was in the possession of a Mrs. Ross who resided in Calumet.

"Someone must have thought the dog resembled Sally," Miss Warrington went on. "Of course, one can't say definitely for no description is given. I've been thinking of driving over there to inquire."

"Why don't you?" suggested Louise quickly.

"It is such a long distance that I dread making the trip alone. I rather hoped I might induce you girls to accompany me."

"We'd like nothing better," declared Jean. "Louise, you're a persuasive talker. Why not telephone Mrs. Crandall and ask her permission?"

Within a few minutes the older Dana girl returned to the living room to report that the headmistress had consented to the request.

"Good!" exclaimed Evangeline. "I'll give the chauffeur the day off and drive a small sedan myself. It will be pleasant being alone— just the three of us."

Before starting the girls put warm fur robes into the auto for the weather was cold. As they drove along flakes of snow began to bank against the windshield. The wiper, though clearing them away, had to be run continuously.

"It looks as if it might storm badly before we get home," Louise said anxiously.

"I hope it doesn't turn into a blizzard," added Jean thoughtfully.

"Oh, we'll be snug and warm in the car," declared Evangeline. "I have had a lot of driving experience, so you needn't be afraid of an accident."

As the car raced through open country the young woman's spirits lifted.

"It's fun to go off this way without being watched every instant," she confided. "When Father was home he never would allow me to drive my own car alone. Always worrying."

"Why was that?" questioned Jean alertly.

"Oh, he feared kidnapers might spirit me off somewhere," the young woman replied with a laugh.

The remark gave Jean and Louise uneasy feelings. Too late they realized that Evangeline had acted rashly in dismissing the chauffeur for the day. She might be in actual danger had her departure from the estate been observed by unscrupulous watchers.

"It seems to me you are taking too great a risk," Louise told Miss Warrington gravely. "You should not be driving like this."

"Oh, I'm not worried."

"If you should be recognized by newspaper reporters or photographers you certainly will be annoyed by them."

"I hadn't thought of that."

"Why don't you disguise yourself?" Louise proposed. "We could stop somewhere along the road and buy anything you need to change your appearance.''

The idea appealed to the young woman. At the next town she located a shop where she was able to purchase an old-fashioned dress, an outdated hat and a pair of horn-rimmed glasses.

''You look exactly like a prim school teacher of thirty years ago!'' laughed Jean as Evangeline came out of the dressing room of the store wearing her new attire. ''No one would recognize you in that outfit.''

The journey was resumed. As the car approached Calumet hours later the girls noticed the rugged terrain of the territory. Miss Warrington mentioned that the mountains were not far away.

''I think we should stop and have an early lunch,'' the young woman proposed as the car entered the outskirts of the city. ''Let's try this restaurant.''

She parked the car in front of a building with a large electric sign advertising meals and the girls went inside. The place was deserted except for a group of men who occupied a table at the rear. They wore hunting attire.

Miss Warrington and the Danas gave their orders to a waitress. The room was so quiet they could not avoid overhearing the conversation of the other group. One of the hunters was relating a recent experience to his companions.

"I was over on Kaleman's Mountain yesterday afternoon looking for deer," he said. "No luck. It was cold, and I felt pretty uncomfortable. Finally I decided I would stop at a cabin along the way, warm myself, and see if I could get some tobacco from the people there."

"What sort of a yarn is this, Thomas?" laughed one of the hunters.

"Nothing very exciting, but it happens to be true, which is more than I can say for your tales," retorted the first speaker good-naturedly. "Well, I knocked on the door. A gruff individual answered but he wouldn't let me inside his shack."

"He probably didn't like your looks, Thomas!" drolled one of his companions.

"Maybe not, but he said he couldn't let me into the place because he was taking care of a crazy man and didn't want anything to happen!"

"Say, you're kidding us."

"No, the story is true," the other insisted seriously. "He wouldn't sell me any tobacco so I went on to the next lodge."

"Thomas is the one who is crazy," joked another hunter. "He's always thinking up tall yarns."

The men began to argue good-naturedly, but the first speaker insisted that his story was true. This opinion was shared by the three young women from Penfield. They were inclined to believe that the hunter had not been joking.

"Perhaps we've stumbled upon a clue," Jean whispered to her companions. "It's quite possible that Mr. Warrington is being held a prisoner in that mountain cabin!"

Louise and Evangeline shared the girl's opinion, both agreeing that the information should be investigated as soon as possible.

"We can't afford to overlook any item," Louise declared soberly.

"How could we ever find the place?" the missing man's daughter questioned in bewilderment. "If I tell those hunters who I am and ask for information the tale soon will be spread that Father has been kidnaped."

"We must try to avoid publicity," Louise nodded. "Let's wait until the group leave the restaurant, then speak with that one man alone. If we are clever he'll not learn your identity."

Hastening through their own luncheon, the girls were alert and waiting when the hunters arose from the table.

"Just tell them that you are searching for a lost relative," Jean instructed Miss Warrington as they followed the men outside.

"You girls do the talking," the young woman whispered nervously. "If necessary, tell that man the entire story, even my true name. I must learn the location of the cabin at any cost!"

CHAPTER XV

An Important Clue

LOUISE AND JEAN waited until the hunters had paid their bills and started from the place. Choosing a moment when the one man had separated himself from his companions they went over and spoke quietly to him.

"I beg your pardon," began Jean, "we couldn't help overhearing your conversation. You were telling your friends about a man who is being detained in a mountainside cabin. Is it a true story?"

"Yes, it is, although I couldn't seem to make the boys believe it."

"We have a friend with us," spoke up Louise, indicating Miss Warrington, "who is searching for a lost relative. When we heard your story we thought instantly that we might have found a clue."

"That's possible," agreed the man though without conviction. "I know it surprised me to find smoke coming from the chimney of the cabin. The last time I was on the mountain the place was deserted."

"Can you tell us how to reach the shack?" Jean asked eagerly.

"I'll draw a rough map for you," the hunter offered.

Taking an old envelope from his pocket, he made a pencil sketch showing the location of the cabin as well as directions for getting there.

"Now this may not be absolutely accurate," he said, "but you should be able to find the place."

"Thank you very much," said the girls as the man left to join his friends.

The hunter had neglected to introduce himself, but on the envelope where he had drawn the crude map there appeared the name of Thomas Farley.

"I wonder if that is the person we were talking to," mused Louise.

"There's no address. Do you suppose he lives near here?" queried Louise.

"No way of telling," Jean replied. "Hunters sometimes travel long distances."

After the girls had returned to their car Evangeline proposed that they start at once for the mountainside shack.

"It will be a long trip and it's growing colder," said Louise, frowning. "We're not prepared to face very bad weather."

"We should have brought warmer wraps," added Jean, supporting her sister.

"But if it is Father who is being held prisoner in the cabin I must release him at once!"

"It won't be that easy," warned Louise soberly. "We would accomplish nothing by walking into a trap. We should make careful plans."

"It's quite possible we'll have a long, hard ride without any results," went on Jean persuasively. "After all, we're only following a vague clue based on the story of a stranger."

"Yes, you are right," Miss Warrington admitted reluctantly. "What do you think we should do next?"

"Let's accomplish our original purpose first of all," suggested Louise, "and find the dog. Then we can discuss our next move."

"All right," agreed her companion.

After making inquiries at a drugstore the girls drove to the poorer section of Calumet where they located the home of Mrs. Ross. The cottage was little more than an unpainted shack, affording a depressing view of the city's mills. Three children, clean but scantily dressed for such cold weather, were playing in the front yard with a large dog.

"That looks like Sally!" exclaimed Miss Warrington. "And it is, too!"

When she called the dog by name, the pet bounded to his mistress, licking her hand and showing great pleasure at seeing her again.

"You seem to be well-fed, Sally," laughed the

young woman. "They must have given you
plenty to eat here."

"Sure," spoke up one of the little boys, staring at the newcomers. "We wouldn't let a dog
go hungry as long as we had anything for ourselves."

"That's what Mom said," spoke up another
red-cheeked youngster.

"Is your mother in the house?" inquired
Louise with a smile.

"I'll call her," offered the first child.

The boy rushed up the front steps. Flinging
open the front door he shouted:

"Hey, Mom! Come on out. Some folks are
here for the dog!"

A thin, hollow-eyed woman in a patched dress
hastened to admit the girls. They stepped into
an immaculate though somewhat scantily furnished living room.

"Just a minute 'til I snap off the electric
iron," Mrs. Ross said, excusing herself.

As the woman vanished into the kitchen the
girls caught a glimpse of a huge basket of un-
ironed clothing. They surmised that she did
laundry work for other people to help support
her little family.

"She is a busy mother," commented Jean.

"Won't you sit down?" Mrs. Ross asked, returning a moment later.

"No, thank you, we came in response to an

advertisement which appeared in the Calumet paper," replied Miss Warrington. "The dog you found ran away from my home several days ago. Her name is Sally."

"You're sure the animal belongs to you?" queried the woman.

"Oh, yes, I couldn't be mistaken. And you see, Sally knows me. She is a blue ribbon dog so I am very glad to get her back."

"You may have the animal by paying for the newspaper advertisement. I wouldn't ask it, only we haven't much money. My husband died a year ago and since then we've had a hard time to make both ends meet."

The girls felt very sorry for the woman.

"I'll do more than pay for the advertisement," said Miss Warrington instantly. "I want to give you a reward for being so honest and for taking such good care of Sally."

"Oh, no," protested the woman. "I couldn't accept any money."

"But why not? I am sure you can use it."

"It wouldn't be right to take it from you, Miss. Now if you were one of these rich ladies with so much money she doesn't know what to do with it I should feel differently."

Miss Warrington coughed in embarrassment. In her clever disguise she had been mistaken for a poor person. She knew of no way to make the woman feel right about accepting the money without revealing her true identity, and that she did not wish to do. She looked toward the Danas for an answer to her problem.

Before the matter could be discussed further, the children burst into the house. They were followed closely by a brown-haired, rather sharp-eyed man in a gray business suit.

"Mom, here's somebody who says the dog belongs to him!" announced the little boy.

"Good afternoon, ma'am," said the stranger, doffing his hat to Mrs. Ross. "My name is Hayward, Jack Hayward. I saw your advertisement in the paper and have come to take my dog away."

"I am afraid you are mistaken," broke in Miss Warrington. "The dog belongs to me."

Jack Hayward looked coolly at the young woman. "I guess I know my own pet when I see it," he retorted. "Here, Fan! Come here!"

The dog backed away as the man approached, walking over to stand instead beside Miss Warrington.

"I guess that proves whose dog she is!" exclaimed the young woman triumphantly.

Louise and Jean nodded in agreement.

"How about it?" demanded the man, turning to Mrs. Ross. "Who gets the animal?"

"Well, these girls were here first—" the woman returned uneasily.

"That should have nothing to do with it. The dog is mine!"

"She doesn't seem to recognize you," Mrs.

Ross answered, her voice taking on a firm note. "No, I shall give the dog to the girls."

"Oh, thank you," beamed Miss Warrington. "And you must accept a reward."

Again Mrs. Ross protested, but Jean, who stood close to the woman, whispered that her companion was well able to pay. The words were louder than she had intended them to be. While he gave no indication he had heard the words, Jack Hayward had not missed the remark. Secretly he made up his mind to make use of the information and if possible gain possession of the pure-bred Great Dane.

"All right, if that's your final decision," he said irritably to Mrs. Ross. "You're making a big mistake, though."

After the man had departed Miss Warrington gave the woman fifty dollars, insisting it was not too much to pay for the return of such a valuable dog.

"Thank you, thank you," Mrs. Ross murmured gratefully. "This money will give the children a wonderful Christmas, but I don't feel right about taking so much."

As the girls led Sally to the car, snow began to fall again.

"I think we should start for home without delay," declared Louise anxiously. "With this wind blowing the roads soon may have snow drifting over them and driving will be dangerous."

Although Miss Warrington still was reluctant to leave the vicinity without trying to locate the mountain cabin, she realized conditions were not favorable for such a trip.

"Yes, we'll go back to Penfield," she agreed. "Jump into the car, Sally."

The three girls sat in front, while the dog occupied the back. The animal's chain was made fast to the coat rail. For a few minutes Sally was restless but soon quieted down and went to sleep on the floor.

Snow continued falling steadily, banking against the windshield. Twice Louise was forced to get out and clear it away when the automatic wiper failed to do the work.

"We were very wise to start for home," Miss Warrington acknowledged before they had traveled very far. "A layer of ice has formed under the snow. I don't dare to drive fast."

"Would you like me to relieve you at the wheel?" volunteered Jean.

"No, thank you, I'll manage. We'll not skid unless I am compelled to put on the brake suddenly," replied the young woman.

Unnoticed by the three girls, a blue coupe had followed them from Calumet. As they approached a steep hill it rapidly drew nearer. Hearing a sharp warning of its horn Miss Warrington quickly pulled over to her side of the road.

"That driver shouldn't attempt to pass me

here," she said nervously. "Doesn't he see that truck coming?"

Instead of passing the sedan, the blue car drew alongside, then crowded on the left. To avoid getting the fenders scraped Miss Warrington was forced to pull over dangerously close to a ditch on the right.

"What *is* that driver trying to do?" Jean demanded angrily.

Peering out the window she recognized the man as Jack Hayward.

"I believe he's deliberately forcing us off of the road!" she exclaimed. "Be careful!" she shouted.

Her warning came too late. The rear tires of her car struck a strip of ice, and the car skidded slightly. With Jack Hayward's coupe pressing close on the left hand side there was nothing Miss Warrington could do to prevent disaster. The rear end of the sedan swung around and slipped into the deep ditch.

CHAPTER XVI

The Chase

The car struck the bottom of the hollow with a hard impact but did not overturn. Miss Warrington was thrown against the steering wheel while Louise and Jean were jolted severely.

"Is anyone hurt?" gasped the heiress when she had recovered her breath.

"I'm all right," murmured Louise. "Only got a bump on my head."

Jean had escaped with minor scratches. In the rear seat Sally was making a great commotion, but a quick investigation satisfied the girls that the dog had not received any injuries. However, she could not be quieted and kept tugging at her chain trying to get away from her prison.

With the car tilted at a severe angle the girls had difficulty in opening the door. As they succeeded in forcing it, they saw that both the blue coupe and the truck had stopped a short distance down the road.

"This accident was that man's fault!" Jean said angrily. "I believe he deliberately pushed us off the road."

"He was quite provoked because Evangeline

135

wouldn't give up Sally," added Louise, struggling out of the automobile. She reached back to offer her sister a helping hand.

The truck driver, a burly fellow in coarse garments thickly padded for warmth came running toward the girls.

"I saw the accident," he declared. "It was the fault of that guy in the blue coupe. He pushed you into the ditch."

Mr. Hayward walked at a deliberate, slow pace toward the group.

"Too bad," he said, surveying the sedan with obvious satisfaction. "You took a nasty skid. Must have struck some ice."

"You forced me into the ditch!" Miss Warrington accused the man.

"I forced you?" the fellow echoed in pretended astonishment. "My dear young lady, I wasn't within a yard of your car when I passed it. You can't blame this accident on me—not in any way."

"The lady's right," interrupted the truck driver. "You shoved her into this spot and it looked to me as if you might have done it on purpose."

"You keep out of this!" Mr. Hayward said curtly. "No one asked for your opinion."

"You got it, anyway."

"I know I am in the right," said Miss Warrington quickly, "but I'll not argue about it.

No great amount of damage has been done. If only I can get the car out of the ditch, I'll be satisfied.''

"I'll help you, Miss," offered the truckman. "Wait and I'll give you a tow."

As he turned away Jean suddenly cried out that Sally was loose. In some manner the chain had become unfastened. Before anyone could prevent it, the dog had leaped from the car and started racing down the road.

Jack Hayward took up the pursuit, soon catching the end of the dragging chain. To everyone's surprise, instead of returning the dog he kept on with her toward his own coupe.

"Why, he's stealing Sally!" cried Miss Warrington. "Of all the high-handed tricks!"

"Hey, you!" shouted the truck driver, starting after the man. "What's the big idea? Come back here!"

Hayward did not pause, but he was no match for the big fellow and was overtaken as he attempted to get into his car.

"Oh, no, you don't!" The truck driver whirled the man about by the shoulder. "Let me have that dog, you low-down——"

"Keep your distance!"

To the horror of Miss Warrington and the Dana girls, Hayward whipped out a revolver. But the truck driver, a former pugilist, was not to be intimidated. His fist shot out, catching

Hayward squarely under the jaw. He staggered back, dropping Sally's chain and the menacing revolver.

Jean seized the weapon, but she was not quick enough to catch Sally's chain before the dog had darted down the road. The pursuit was taken up by both Louise and Evangeline, but they had to abandon it as the Great Dane leaped a fence and ran into a near-by woods.

The girls came back to the car to find Hayward lying on the ground where he had fallen. He was unconscious.

"Oh, I hope he isn't hurt seriously," Miss Warrington murmured anxiously.

"He ain't hurt none, lady," answered the truck driver carelessly. "Just knocked out cold. He'll be around in a few minutes."

"We can't leave him here on the road," protested Louise.

"Right you are," nodded the man.

Picking up the victim as easily as if the load were a sack of flour, he tossed Hayward into the seat of the blue coupe.

"Now let's get the car out of the ditch, young ladies," he urged. "I'm kind of in a hurry. Want to reach Calumet before the roads get any worse."

Jean already had returned to the Warrington auto, where she gingerly had hidden Hayward's revolver in the pocket of the back seat. Not until the car had been pulled from the ditch and the

girls were ready to start on again did she reveal
what she had done.

"Do you think we should keep the weapon?"
Louise questioned doubtfully.

"Why not? It certainly would be the height
of folly to return it to Mr. Hayward. He might
try to use it again."

"Yes, that's so," Louise acknowledged. "He
is a dangerous character."

"For all we know he may be wanted by the
police for some crime," reasoned Jean as she
took paper and pencil from her pocket. "I'm
going to take down the license number of his
car."

The girls thanked the truck driver for helping
them. When Miss Warrington offered the man
money for his services, he promptly refused it.

"It was a real pleasure giving that guy a biff
on the chin," he said, grinning broadly. "Well,
so long. I hope you find your dog."

After some discussion the girls decided to al-
ter their route back to Penfield. Instead of following the main road they turned into a narrow,
twisting highway which led in the direction Sally
had gone. There was a possible chance, they
thought, that they might catch a glimpse of the
runaway dog.

Miss Warrington drove very slowly for a
time, frequently getting out of the car to call her
pet's name and whistle for her.

"It's no use," she said at last. "Sally is gone

and this time I doubt I'll ever find her again," she added dolefully.

"Maybe she went back to Mrs. Ross's place," said Louise hopefully.

"Why don't we stop at the next town and mail a card, asking the woman to be on the lookout for Sally?" suggested Jean.

The idea appealed to Evangeline. "Since Mrs. Ross has no telephone, let's do that," she said.

At the little village of Cordville the three alighted and entered the post office. While her companions were composing the message, Louise noticed that the postmaster was tacking a poster on the wall. Curiously she went over to look at the photograph of someone wanted by the police.

"Jean! Eve!" she exclaimed, motioning to them. "Will you look at this!"

The poster bore a likeness to Jack Hayward and stated that a reward was being offered for the man's apprehension as a swindler.

"Do you suppose he is the same person?" murmured Jean in astonishment.

"It looks exactly like him," maintained Louise. "Notice the profile. Hayward had a slight bump on his nose just as the one in this picture," she added.

"Then we've allowed a wanted criminal to escape!" exclaimed Miss Warrington. "How stupid of us."

"He hasn't escaped yet," declared Louise with decision. "We'll notify the police immediately, and they may be able to catch him."

Luck was with the girls for they found a state traffic patrolman in the town. In order that no time would be lost in locating Hayward they guided the officer back to the scene of the auto accident.

Unfortunately the blue coupe had disappeared. It was not possible to tell which of the forked roads the driver had taken for snow had covered his tracks.

"At least we have the license number of the car," said Jean, offering it to the patrolman, at the same time giving him the revolver. "These may help you in your search."

Louise had noticed a group of children skating on a near-by pond. Thinking she might obtain information from them she walked over to the rink and questioned one of the older boys.

"Sure, I saw a blue coupe drive away not ten minutes ago," he told her. "It turned down the left hand road over there."

Quickly the girl hastened back with the news, only to learn that the officer had driven away. He had not followed the road indicated.

"Oh, dear, he'll never catch the man now," she said in disappointment. "Should we try to trace him ourselves?"

"Yes, let's do," agreed Evangeline without an instant's hesitation. "Nothing would please me more than to see that man behind bars."

The girls traveled ten miles without overtaking a car which even resembled the one they sought. Then, as they toured through a small city, Jean suddenly pointed to a coupe which stood in front of a restaurant.

"That looks like it! Stop your car!"

Miss Warrington brought her sedan to a halt only a short distance beyond the eating place. Quickly Jean compared the license number with the one which she had copied down, and was elated to find that it was the same as the one on the coupe.

"It's Hayward's car," she declared in satisfaction. "Now to catch him!"

Hurriedly alighting, the girls crossed the street to the restaurant and glanced through the plate glass window. They could see the man they sought drinking a cup of coffee at the lunch counter within.

"It's Hayward, all right," announced Jean with conviction.

"You and Evangeline stay here and keep watch," directed Louise. "I'll go for the police. Just be careful the man doesn't catch a glimpse of you and rush away."

She disappeared down the street but was gone less than ten minutes. To Jean and her companion who nervously waited it seemed fully an hour. They breathed sighs of relief as they saw her hastening back, accompanied by two husky policemen.

"There is your man," Louise indicated, pointing out Hayward. "At least we think he is wanted as a swindler. He resembles the picture which was posted, and he carried a revolver."

"He's the man we're after," agreed one of the officers grimly. "Fits the description perfectly. Nice work, young lady."

"He'll probably try to resist arrest unless he's taken by surprise," said Jean anxiously.

"We'll handle him."

Warning the girls to keep out of the way and avoid trouble, the officers made certain Hayward did not notice them. Then quietly they entered the building to get their man.

CHAPTER XVII

A Scoop

An instant before the policemen stepped inside the restaurant, Jack Hayward turned his head and saw the Dana girls through the plate glass window. Warned of impending arrest, he jumped down from the high stool at the counter and made a rush for the rear exit.

The door stuck fast. Although he jerked frantically at it he could not open it. An officer seized him, clapping handcuffs on the man's wrists.

"Why are you arresting me?" Hayward whined. "It wasn't my fault the girls' car went off into the ditch. But if any damage was done I'm willing to pay for it."

"We haven't heard anything about damage being done to a car," he was told curtly. "You're wanted on another charge. Come along."

The man was hustled to Police Headquarters, still protesting his innocence. The three girls at the request of the officers went along to offer the information they had regarding the prisoner. After telling all they knew about the man, the girls waited while the police searched the files for his record.

"Jack Hayward seems to be his latest alias," remarked the captain, studying a card. "Real name is Mortimer Kaner."

"Kaner!" exclaimed Jean, wondering if she had heard correctly.

"Right. He's a fairly well-known character in police records. Fake bond selling is one of his specialties."

"It seems to me I've heard my father mention that someone who used to work for him had a brother by the name of Mortimer," Miss Warrington murmured reflectively.

"And what is your name?" the captain shot at the young woman unexpectedly.

As Miss Warrington did not wish to give her family name for publicity, she mentioned the first one that entered her mind.

"Eve—Eve Ring," she said. "I'd like to speak to the man if I may."

"It will be all right," was the reply. "Hendon, take these young women to the prisoner."

A policeman came forward and escorted the three girls to a private room where Mortimer Kaner was undergoing rigid questioning. At first the man would have nothing to say, but as Louise and Jean interposed a few inquiries of their own, being careful not to reveal Miss Warrington's identity, he reluctantly admitted that Nat Kaner was indeed his brother.

"Where is he now?" Louise persisted.

"I don't know," the prisoner returned sullenly. "Haven't seen him in over a year."

While the girls did not believe the man spoke the truth, they realized they could learn nothing more by questioning him further. As they already had been away from home much longer than they had intended, they left the police station, resuming their journey in a blinding snowstorm. Later, as the sedan rolled through the gateway into the estate grounds, Miss Warrington remarked that the day had been a tiring though exciting one.

"I only hope our clue regarding Father leads to something tangible," she said anxiously. "I'll telephone Detective McCarter at once and consult with him about what step to take next."

The man promised to come at once. While waiting for him, the Danas discussed the situation of Mortimer Kaner. They realized that the man's arrest soon would be public knowledge.

"I wish the *Evening Journal* here could get the news before the *Post* does," Jean remarked. "It would serve brazen Abe Mantel right to be scooped."

"Why don't we see to it that he is?" proposed Louise mischievously. "All we need to do is telephone the *Journal* editor and give him a tip. He should be able to get his own story then."

No sooner was the idea conceived than it was put into effect. The man was very appreciative.

Jean had just finished talking with the newspaper man when Detective McCarter arrived at the mansion. He listened with flattering attention to the Dana girls' story of their sleuthing around Calumet, and examined the crude map drawn for them by the hunter.

"This clue certainly is worth tracing down," he said. "I'll get over there as soon as I can. But first I plan to interview Mortimer Kaner. I feel certain he knows his brother's whereabouts."

"Since you have so much work to do," said Louise quickly, "why not let us investigate the mountain cabin for you? If it should prove to be a false lead we should feel bad about having taken up so much of your time."

The detective bestowed a knowing smile upon the girls, for he surmised that they were eager to embark upon an adventure as well as to help him.

"Very well, I'll give you the first chance," he said. "The clue is yours so you deserve an opportunity to work on it. I'm not keen about adventure," he smiled, "only in locating Mr. Warrington."

Louise and Jean appreciated the man's attitude, and determined that they would do everything in their power to assist him. Immediately they began to discuss plans with Miss Warrington for a return visit to Calumet the following day to begin their investigation.

"We can get everything ready and make an early start tomorrow morning," said Louise, "if the weather favors us and Mrs. Crandall doesn't object to us going.''

"Let's get back to Starhurst right away and talk with her,'' Jean proposed.

Miss Warrington placed her car and chauffeur at the disposal of the Dana girls. In the center of Penfield they made a brief stop to purchase warm undergarments which they knew would be needed for the following day's journey into the mountains.

Observing that the *Evening Journal* had an extra upon the street, Jean purchased a copy. Eagerly she and her sister spread out the paper on the car seat, scanning the large, black head-lines.

"It's here!'' Louise chuckled triumphantly. "The story we telephoned to the *Journal* office. They played it up big. Kaner is really an important criminal if he can rate an extra.''

"Our names figure,'' Jean murmured as she read. "We're given credit for the capture. I didn't count on that.''

"The editor must have obtained the facts directly from the police station. Don't you wish you could see Abe Mantel's face when he reads the story?'' laughed Louise. "I do.''

"Make a wish and it may come true,'' laughed Jean, indicating a young man who was walking down the street toward the car. "Here comes Abe Mantel now, and his face looks as black as a thunder cloud.''

"Probably he has read the story," chuckled Louise. "I'm sure his tabloid missed getting an account of the arrest."

As the man reached a point almost directly opposite the limousine, Lettie Briggs chanced to come out of the corner drugstore. She failed to observe the Dana girls, but paused as she saw the reporter and coughed loudly.

"Oh, hello, Mr. Mantel," she greeted him in a simpering voice.

The reporter paused and faced the girl squarely. "A fine newspaper person you turned out to be! I thought you told me you were experienced!"

"Why, what is wrong?"

"Take a look at this!" Angrily the man thrust a copy of the *Evening Journal* under the girl's eyes. "I nearly lost my job on account of the opposition getting a scoop!"

"I—I don't understand."

"You wouldn't," Abe Mantel retorted harshly. "You were supposed to keep me posted on the doings of the Dana girls and their connection with the Warringtons. Just see this story!"

"I don't know anything about a Mortimer Kaner," Lettie said in bewilderment. "Louise and Jean were gone all day."

"Of course they were! They were over at Calumet. Couldn't you have kept track of them?"

"I don't see how. Mrs. Crandall never lets me get very far out of her sight," she said crossly. Then she brightened. "Maybe if I tell her I am on the staff of the *Post* she might be more lenient," she added importantly.

"Well, tell her that," said the reporter without meaning what he said. "Tell the old girl anything you like. Only keep close watch of Louise and Jean Dana. Another slip like this one and I'll be without a job."

Lettie beamed from ear to ear, assuming that Abe Mantel had offered her a paying position on the Penfield newspaper.

"Oh, thanks," she said gratefully. "I'll try to follow the Dana girls after this whenever they leave the dormitory. I've always wanted to be a reporter!"

"All right, this is your chance. Telephone to me if you learn anything important." Abe Mantel started away, then added, "But mind, no more tall tales about sable coats! I got a nice calling down on account of that story."

Just then, before the reporter could go farther down the street, the Warrington chauffeur started the engine of the limousine. Startled, Lettie and Mantel both turned to stare at the occupants of the back seat.

"Well, of all the sneaking tricks!" Lettie exclaimed furiously. "The Dana girls have been listening to our conversation!"

CHAPTER XVIII

The Lost Map

LOUISE AND JEAN remained undisturbed by the accusations for their consciences were clear.

"Sorry, Lettie," said Jean coolly. "Did you expect us to blow a siren to inform you that we happen to be here?"

Ignoring his companion, Abe Mantel moved quickly to the curb. He smiled at the girls in what he vainly thought was an engaging way.

"How do you do?" he said, doffing his hat. "Isn't this the Warrington limousine you are riding in?"

"Yes, it is," replied Louise guardedly.

"Nice to be so friendly with rich folks," the reporter went on. "By the way, what's doing at the estate?"

"Really, I couldn't tell you," returned the older Dana girl.

"They haven't found any trace of Mr. Warrington yet?" the man inquired.

"Is that so?" inquired Jean mischievously, acting as if the reporter had made a statement instead of asking a question.

"See here," said Abe Mantel, losing his temper, "you girls know plenty about the case if

151

only you would talk! It wouldn't surprise me if you are responsible for the *Evening Journal* scooping our paper today!"

"Why, whatever gave you such an idea!" laughed Jean mockingly. "I fear you just aren't a very good gatherer of news, Mr. Mantel."

Louise signaled to the driver and the limousine drove away, leaving Lettie and the reporter standing at the curb. Upon their arrival at the dormitory a surprise awaited the Dana girls. As they opened the door to their suite a visitor quickly arose from a chair by the window.

"Aunt Harriet!" exclaimed Jean, running to give her relative a kiss. "This is a surprise."

"Have you been waiting long for us?" Louise inquired anxiously. "Why didn't you write you were coming? We certainly would have been here to meet you," she added.

"I came only an hour ago," laughed Miss Dana. "I didn't write because I had no idea of making the trip. This morning a neighbor telephoned she was driving to Penfield and offered to take me along. So here I am!"

"We're so glad to have you!" cried Louise. "Surprises are such fun."

"Do you often miss your classes as you did today?" Miss Dana asked somewhat severely.

"No," Jean said hastily. "Mrs. Crandall gave us permission to leave. We were in Calumet with Miss Warrington."

"And we hope to gain a leave of absence for tomorrow too!" added Louise gaily. "It's really important that we go."

After offering a complete account of their day's adventure the girls spoke of plans for visiting the mountain lodge.

"I'm not certain that I approve," Miss Dana declared soberly. "Even if Mrs. Crandall gives her consent I can't allow you to go there."

"Oh, Aunt Harriet," wailed Jean, "all our plans are made. And both Miss Warrington and Mr. McCarter are counting upon us."

"Wait until I finish speaking, Jean. I meant to say I can't allow you to go there unchaperoned. Now if I were invited——"

"You are!" laughed Louise in relief. "And perhaps you wouldn't mind talking to Mrs. Crandall in our behalf. I'm sure she would be more reasonable if you were to do that."

"Very well," smiled Miss Dana, "I don't mind. I believe I can arrange matters for you —that is, if you're not behind in your studies."

"All of our marks have been good," declared Jean. "We easily can make up everything we might miss for a couple of days."

That very evening the kindly woman consulted the headmistress, obtaining permission for her nieces to be absent from school the following day. Upon hearing the news Lettie and Ina expressed in no uncertain terms their opinion that the Danas again were being shown favoritism.

"It makes me sick," she murmured over and over.

A number of other students might have shared the same belief had not loyal Evelyn Starr spread the word that her friends were traveling to Calumet on a secret mission. Seizing eagerly upon the information, Lettie immediately telephoned to the reporter, Abe Mantel.

"The Dana girls are going somewhere tomorrow on an all-day trip," she repeated to him. "I think they may be starting for the mountains near Calumet. At least they bought a lot of warm clothing to take with them."

"Thanks for the tip," he answered. "I'll be on the watch."

Early the next morning the Warrington limousine with the colored chauffeur at the wheel arrived at the dormitory. Evangeline had come along and greeted Miss Dana cordially.

"Your nieces have been wonderful to me," she said. "A great comfort as well as a great help."

Louise explained that her aunt would accompany the group on the trip.

"That's splendid," exclaimed Miss Warrington. "I'll feel so much better having a person of experience go with us. We'll probably need a chaperon."

"I may be more of a nuisance than a helper," the woman responded. "However, I hope to keep my nieces from doing anything rash."

According to the map drawn up by the hunter,

it would not be possible to reach the mountain
lodge by automobile. Therefore, the girls
planned to motor to the nearest point and hike
the remaining distance.

"I haven't told the chauffeur why we are going to the mountains," Evangeline confided to
her companions as the car moved away from the
school entrance. "George is very superstitious
and might start to imagine all sorts of things."

"We'll be careful not to divulge anything,"
promised Jean in a whisper.

The journey to Calumet threatened to con-
sume more time than the girls had anticipated,
for the roads were covered with snow drifts.
Twice the chauffeur was compelled to get out of
the car and shovel in order to clear the way.
While Miss Dana and the girls remained snug
and warm in the heated auto, they were alarmed
at the frequent delays.

"We're eager to reach the mountains early in
the day," Miss Warrington said to the colored
man. "Can't we go faster?"

"Not unless you all wants to land in a ditch,"
he replied. "These roads is mighty slick, Miss
Evangeline."

"Then you are wise not to hurry," the young
woman agreed with a sigh. "Only I wish we had
started earlier."

Very few automobiles had traveled over the
highway in the past twenty-four hours. However, shortly after leaving Penfield, Jean

glanced through the rear window and observed that a dark blue coupe was following close behind them.

"I think that driver wants to go around us," she said to the chauffeur.

George pulled over toward the snowbank on the right, giving the blue car ample room to pass in the narrow track. Instead of taking advantage of the opportunity, the other driver immediately slackened his pace.

"You may as well go ahead, George," instructed Miss Warrington. "Apparently the fellow doesn't wish to go around us. He may be afraid of slipping into the ditch on the left."

When Jean looked back every now and then the car still would be following. Occasionally it would creep fairly close, although never near enough for her to obtain a clear view of the driver.

"You don't suppose that fellow could be trailing us intentionally?" she asked uneasily.

"It's not likely," responded Miss Dana carelessly. "No doubt he is a timid driver who is afraid of the icy roads."

Presently as the Warrington car rounded a bend Louise said casually to Evangeline:

"May I look at the map a moment, please? You have it?"

A look of consternation came over Miss Warrington's face.

"No, I didn't bring it, Louise. I don't even

remember having possession of it. Didn't you take it with you just as you were leaving my home yesterday?"

"Not that I recall. How about you, Jean?" her sister asked.

"I haven't it."

To be certain they were making no mistake, the three girls searched through their pocket-books, but the missing paper could not be located. Both Jean and Louise had a vague recollection that Evangeline had offered the paper to them, yet they could not recall actually having carried it away from Warrington Manor.

"We haven't much chance of finding the mountain lodge without a map," declared Jean in discouragement. "What shall we do?"

"We'll have to turn back and try to locate the paper," decided Louise. "It would be foolish to go on."

"George, stop the car!" ordered Miss Warrington through the speaking tube. "We are turning back at once."

Startled by the urgent tone of the young woman's voice, George, without glancing into the reflecting mirror, slammed on the foot brake. The limousine stopped with a sudden lurch, throwing its passengers forward.

"Look out!" screamed Jean fearfully.

Her warning was spoken too late. Suddenly the blue coupe which had been following so close plunged into the rear of the Warrington car.

CHAPTER XIX

COSTLY DELAY

THE force of the collision flung Jean and Miss Dana from the car seat, but neither was injured. They were aided to their feet by Louise and Evangeline. Everyone alighted to learn the extent of the damage to the limousine.

"Are you all right, Aunt Harriet?" Louise inquired anxiously.

"Yes," Miss Dana replied, straightening her hat, "no thanks to that man!"

She glanced angrily toward the driver of the blue coupe, a young fellow with light colored hair and mustache. His black felt hat was pulled low over his eyes, partly concealing his face from the woman's gaze.

"Who is that person?" Jean whispered to Louise. "Haven't we seen him before?"

"I think not."

The coupe had struck the limousine squarely from behind. While very little damage had been done to the Warrington car, the smaller automobile, unprotected by strong bumpers, had suffered a crushed radiator shell.

Climbing from the blue auto, the young man came over to the group. All the while he kept his head held so low that his features could not be distinguished.

"Look at my car!" he said in a gruff voice. "This was your fault!"

"Our fault!" echoed Miss Warrington in great amazement.

"Certainly," the young man snapped. "You had no business stopping so suddenly. What was the big idea anyway?"

"We might ask you why you were traveling so closely behind us," replied Evangeline coolly.

"I was trying to get around."

"We gave you an opportunity miles back and you declined to take it. I am sorry, but I can't assume blame for an accident which you caused yourself," she said finally.

The young man might have become increasingly unpleasant, had not a gust of wind whipped his hat from his head at that moment. A look of panic crossed his face and he clapped a hand to his hair. Holding it in that manner he pursued the headgear which was rolling down the road.

"That's funny," murmured Louise. "He must be wearing a wig!"

Capturing his hat the young man pushed it onto his head and returned to the scene of the accident. At once he started for his own battered coupe.

"This whole thing was your fault," he muttered to Miss Warrington, "but I'm willing to forget about it."

George, the colored chauffeur, had heard Louise's pointed remark regarding the man's wig. As the young fellow turned the Warrington driver managed to brush against him, once more dislodging the hat.

"Say, you lug!" the stranger exclaimed wrathfully.

Then he gazed in confusion at the snowy road. There at his feet lay not only the black felt hat but a blond wig. His own black, curly hair was exposed to the scornful gaze of Miss Dana and the three girls.

"Abe Mantel!" cried Jean, recognizing the reporter from the *Post*.

"So you have been following us all the way from Penfield!" exclaimed Louise indignantly. "And you adopted a disguise!"

"I was only obeying orders," the man defended himself. "The editor told me I'd be fired if I didn't bring in a good story. Why not give me a break?" he whined.

"We'll tell you nothing!" Miss Warrington replied coldly. "Now please get your car out of the way so that we may turn around."

"You're going back to Penfield?" the reporter questioned in amazement. "But I thought—" Then he stopped, realizing he had said too much.

"Evidently you thought wrong, young man," spoke up Miss Dana severely. "You may consider yourself fortunate if we don't report you to the police."

"Don't do that," Mantel pleaded. "I'll get my car out of the way."

Hastily he pulled into the shallow, frozen ditch, making room for the limousine to turn

around. As Miss Warrington and her party
drove back toward Penfield, he did not attempt
to follow them.

"We've shaken him off, for the time being at
least," Jean declared, glancing through the car
window. "But if I know Abe Mantel, he'll not
be discouraged for long."

"It was amusing the way George exposed him
by brushing off his hat," chuckled Evangeline.
"How do you suppose Mantel knew we were
starting on this trip?"

"I wonder myself," returned Louise soberly.
"I'm thinking that Lettie Briggs may have given
him a clue. Thank goodness, she didn't know
our exact destination."

"We aren't sure of it ourselves," added Jean.
"What shall we do if we can't find the map?"

"We'll *have* to find it," responded Evangeline with determination. "Father may be held
a prisoner in that mountain cabin. I'll never
rest until I trace down the clue."

By this time a snowplow was at work on the
side roads. Traffic had begun to make the main
highway more open and the trip back to Penfield
was run in fairly good speed. First the girls
went to Warrington Manor, where Evangeline
searched through the desk and every possible
place in which she thought the map might have
been placed. Not a cubbyhole was left unex-
plored.

"It isn't here," she declared at last. "I'm
satisfied I didn't have it."

"Then it must be somewhere in our room at school," decided Louise. "Strange that my mind is such a blank. I can't remember seeing the paper after we showed it to Mr. McCarter."

The entire party drove to Starhurst. While Miss Dana and Evangeline waited in the car for them, Louise and Jean proceeded to turn their room topsy-turvy in a frantic search for the map.

"I'm so disappointed I could cry!" Jean declared in a vexed tone. "After getting such an early start, only to be held up and delayed like this! I don't believe we'll ever find the map. It's gone, I'm positive."

"It certainly isn't anywhere in our room. Try to recall, Jean. What could we have done with it?" Louise mused.

"I've been turning things over in my mind ever since we discovered it was missing. I seem to remember that Evangeline gave the map to us, but I'm not absolutely certain," her sister replied.

"This is the most stupid thing we ever did. It's not like either of us to lose such an important paper."

"You don't suppose Lettie might have had anything to do with its disappearance?" asked Jean.

"I don't see how we can blame our loss on her," Louise replied gloomily. "Still, we've investigated every other possibility."

At that moment Ina Mason chanced to pass

down the hall. Observing the confusion in the Dana suite she paused in the doorway to stare.

"You're not moving out?" she demanded curiously.

"No," smiled Jean ruefully, "nothing like that. We're looking for something we lost."

"A paper," added Louise. "A crudely drawn map. We need it for some work we are doing."

"Why, I saw a scrap of paper lying outside your door last night," remarked Ina.

"You did?" Jean questioned eagerly.

"It looked like an old letter with a few lines drawn on it."

"Yes, that was what we lost!" exclaimed Louise, rushing to the hallway. "I wonder if the corridors have been swept today?"

"It won't do you a bit of good to look," observed Ina in some amusement.

"Why not?" demanded Louise, whirling toward the teasing girl.

"Because the paper is gone. Lettie took it! I saw her."

"Lettie!" exclaimed the Dana girls together.

"I saw her pick up the paper last night. I don't know what she did with it."

"Thanks for telling us," Jean said quickly. "We'll find her right away."

The Danas hurried to Lettie's room, rapping firmly on the door.

"Come in," called the Briggs girl who was propped up on the day bed, reading a novel and nibbling at chocolate candy.

As the Dana girls entered she hastily covered the candy box with a pillow so that she would not be expected to offer any of the confection to her callers.

"Well, this is a surprise," she greeted them mockingly. "Aren't you back early from your trip?"

"Lettie," Jean began abruptly, "Ina tells us you picked up a paper from the hallway last night."

"Perhaps I did. What about it?"

"The paper belonged to us. May we have it, please?"

"I haven't it any more."

"What did you do with it, Lettie?" Louise asked anxiously. "Please tell us. It's extremely important."

"I tore it to pieces."

"Oh, Lettie!" Jean moaned. "Where did you throw them?"

"They're burned up by now. I guess your paper is gone. You ought to take better care of your things and not drop them in the halls!"

Disheartened, Louise and Jean returned to the car to report the news to Miss Warrington and their aunt.

"I don't see what we can do except try to find the cabin without the map," said Jean.

"I have another idea!" exclaimed Louise suddenly. "Why not telephone Thomas Farley whose name was on the envelope?"

"Of course!" cried Evangeline, her face lighting up. "We should have thought of doing that before."

"We're not sure he is the person we spoke to nor that he lives in Calumet," said Jean doubtfully. "But it's worth trying."

Fearful that Ina Mason or the prying Lettie might overhear the conversation, the party motored to Penfield where the Danas telephoned. Louise and Jean tried for over a half hour to connect with the man but finally were compelled to discontinue their attempts.

"No luck," they reported to the others as they came back to the auto.

"There's a chance we might locate Mr. Farley by driving to Calumet," Louise said in a discouraged voice, "but I rather doubt it."

"Can you remember any of the directions for reaching the cabin?" Evangeline asked thoughtfully after a moment.

"From the drawing it appeared to me that it was located about midway up Kaleman's Mountain," answered Jean. "Of course, the map may not have been an accurate one."

"Two main roads went up the mountain," Miss Warrington was able to recall. "Now if only we could remember which one was marked!"

"I know who might help us!" cried Louise suddenly. "Detective McCarter!"

"The very person," agreed the heiress enthusiastically. "Let's telephone to him at once!"

CHAPTER XX

Snowbound

AFTER making three telephone calls Miss Warrington finally located the detective at a Penfield hotel.

"Drive over and I'll talk with you immediately," he promised. "As a matter of fact, I was trying to reach you. I have news for you."

The young woman was hopeful that the detective might have gained a clue as to her father's whereabouts, but in this she was doomed to disappointment. Mr. McCarter's news concerned a recent visit to the cell of Mortimer Kaner.

"I had a long talk with the man last evening," the detective reported. "At first he wouldn't give me any information, but gradually I broke him down. I learned enough to satisfy myself he has been involved in many crooked schemes. It's my opinion too that he has had a part in your father's muddled affairs, Miss Warrington."

"You didn't learn anything which tended to incriminate Father—" the girl began anxiously.

"Quite the contrary. I believe that when everything finally is revealed, it will be proven that your father is innocent of any intention to defraud. The trouble is that he put too much trust in other people."

"Nat Kaner especially," declared Miss Warrington bitterly. "I always tried to warn Father against that man, but he only laughed at me. All the while those two brothers must have been plotting and scheming together!"

"We haven't any proof yet, but I think we shall have it soon. If Mr. Warrington were here he could clear up many points that would help his case."

"I am sure Father did not run away. He is being detained against his will. I hope and pray we'll find him at the cabin on the mountainside," the young woman sighed.

"I don't place much faith in the clue," admitted Mr. McCarter frankly. "When are you starting for Calumet?"

The girls explained about the lost map and the trouble which had resulted.

"Perhaps we can draw up another," said the detective, taking out paper and pencil. "Now let's see. There were two roads and the left hand one was marked."

"Oh, that was what we were trying to remember!" exclaimed Jean in relief. "After we reach the end of the road which direction should we take? Do you recall?"

"I really don't know. I can't seem to recollect a thing about it."

"Well, at least we have something to start on," declared Louise. "If we could reach the end of the road we should be able to locate the cabin without much trouble."

"While I hardly expect that Mr. Warrington is imprisoned there, such may be the case," said the detective. "So be very cautious in your actions. Should your suspicions be aroused, get in touch with me at once. I'll bring the police."

"We'll be very careful," promised Evangeline.

Several hours of valuable time had been lost through the delay. Every member of the party felt relieved when a second start was made.

Always a careful driver, George had put on tire chains. Now, with no danger of skidding, he was able to make better speed than he had earlier in the morning. The side roads remained nearly deserted. Nowhere did the girls see a sign of Abe Mantel's battered blue coupe.

"He got away somehow," Jean reflected.

Mid-afternoon found the party at Calumet once more. When a brief stop was made to refuel, Miss Warrington suggested luncheon at a hotel. Everyone was hungry.

"Does anyone realize what time it is?" she asked, looking at her watch. "It is three-thirty!"

"So late?" asked Louise in dismay. "Darkness will overtake us before many hours."

Fearful that they might not reach the mountain cabin before nightfall, the party hastened through the meal and started on again. Fate seemed to be against them, for they had not driven fifteen miles beyond the city when they were confronted with a huge sign blocking the road.

"A detour," groaned Jean. "No telling how long it is, either."

Snow was banked deep along the sides of the road indicated. The cleared track was so narrow that the limousine crept forward at little more than a snail's pace. Presently George brought the car to a complete standstill.

"Now what?" inquired Miss Warrington impatiently as the colored man got out to brush snow from a post.

"Sorry, Miss Evangeline," the chauffeur reported as he opened the car door, "this road ain't marked. Which way should we go from here?"

Two roads, both of them narrow and twisting, angled away from the point where the limousine stood. Jean and Louise were inclined to take the right one, while their aunt agreed with Evangeline in thinking that the left one should be chosen. Each one led to the mountain ahead.

"Let's try the left one, George," instructed Miss Warrington. "If it doesn't seem to lead anywhere we'll have to turn back."

The chauffeur climbed into the front seat and drove on. For a few miles the road was moderately good, then the cleared track ended. Twice

George nearly stalled the car in the deep snow.

"This can't be the right road," Miss Dana said at last.

"We'll have to turn back," acknowledged Evangeline, glancing anxiously at the darkening sky. "Oh, dear, we've lost so much time."

"We can't turn around here, Miss," said the colored man. "The road am too narrow."

"Then keep on until you find a wide place," instructed Miss Warrington wearily.

The lane wound on for a mile farther. Still there was no place where a turn could be made. Jean glanced at her wrist watch. It was nearly six o'clock.

"It will be dark in a very short while," remarked Miss Dana. "I don't see how we possibly can reach the cabin tonight. I feel that it would be dangerous for us to attempt mountain roads after nightfall."

"We'll have to stop somewhere," agreed Miss Warrington unwillingly. "But apparently we're miles from any town."

"I see something white ahead," observed Jean, staring in the distance.

"That a graveyard," muttered George uneasily. "Bad luck fo' sure. Why I come on this trip anyhow?"

"Now don't start any of your superstitious chatter, George," Evangeline reproved the fellow sternly.

"I was looking beyond the graveyard," resumed Jean who had been interrupted. "I see a farmhouse just over the hill."

"Then let's stop there and try to get food and lodging for the night," Miss Warrington proposed. "Turn in, George, when we come to that place ahead."

The colored chauffeur offered no response, lapsing into a sulky silence. In truth, he feared to remain overnight in such an isolated community. The glimpse of the near-by graveyard had filled him with foreboding. Jean smiled as she saw him slip a hand beneath his coat to finger a rabbit's foot he wore as a charm.

Viewed at close range, the farmhouse appeared somewhat dilapidated. As there was no other habitation within miles the party decided that the place would have to do. Jean and Louise went to the door to inquire if accommodations could be made by the party.

An elderly man with white hair came to the door and invited the girls into the house. He was a kind-looking person.

"Come in, come in," he said heartily. "I'll call my wife. She's getting supper in the kitchen. Oh, Maud!"

A stout woman with a friendly face came hurrying to the living room, wiping her hands on the corner of a blue-checked apron.

"Maud, some folks are here in a car," explained the farmer whose name was Herman Reid. "They took the wrong turn back yonder.

They want to know can they have supper here and rooms for the night?"

"We'll be glad to pay for everything," Jean interposed quickly.

"Why yes, we can keep you," the woman said, hesitating only an instant. "We're not much fixed for having company, though."

"Oh, we don't want anything fancy," declared Louise. "Just plain food and a place to sleep will be quite all right."

"How many are there in your party?"

"Five of us, counting the chauffeur," Jean replied.

"You're traveling with a chauffeur!" Mrs. Reid exclaimed. "Oh, I don't know whether I could keep him or not. I have only two spare rooms."

"I'm sure George wouldn't mind sleeping somewhere downstairs," Louise replied.

"Is he honest?"

"I'm sure George wouldn't steal anything."

"Maybe it would be better to put him in the barn," the woman said, frowning.

"Now Maud," protested her husband, "it's right cold out there and the poor fellow might freeze."

"George is rather superstitious too," added Jean hastily. "He might be afraid and think he was seeing ghosts if he should stay outside."

"I'll make up a bed for him in the kitchen," Mrs. Reid decided at last. "Tell your folks to

come inside. Herman, you help the ladies in
while I cook up some victuals.''

The farmhouse was not furnished comfortably, but cheerful fires smoldered on the hearths.
The hospitality of the kindly couple more than
compensated for any missing luxuries. Miss
Dana and the girls thoroughly enjoyed the plain
but well-cooked supper which was served to
them in the warm kitchen.

''You must live a peaceful, happy life here in
the country,'' Miss Warrington remarked cheerfully. ''I almost envy you your privacy.''

''It isn't always so pleasant being snow-
bound,'' returned Mrs. Reid. ''We have our
troubles too.'' Her eyes took on a sad expression as she spoke.

''We're only renters,'' admitted the farmer.
''I'd like to buy the place but things haven't
gone so well with us the past three years. Bad
crops and a string of minor disasters.''

''Now don't get started on that, Herman,''
spoke his wife with a warning glance. ''We
manage pretty well as it is.''

The Reids would say nothing further concerning their difficulties. At an early hour everyone went to bed.

As dawn broke the entire household stirred to
life once more. Mrs. Reid prepared a hearty
breakfast of cereal, toast, ham, potatoes and
coffee. How good it tasted!

''My, I haven't eaten this much in years,''

Miss Warrington laughed apologetically. "How much do we owe you, Mrs. Reid, for everything?"

"Nothing at all. My husband and I are glad to have had you as our guests."

"Oh, but I insist upon paying," replied Miss Warrington. "Won't you mention a price?"

"Well, if you insist. Would two dollars be too much?"

The young woman smiled at the words. Taking a bill from her purse she thrust it into the woman's hand.

"You've made a mistake!" Mrs. Reid protested. "This is a fifty-dollar bill."

"I know it is."

"We haven't any change."

"You are to keep it all, Mrs. Reid."

The woman demurred. Then, as Miss Warrington insisted in her wish, tears of gratitude shone in Mrs. Reid's eyes.

"Thank you very much," she murmured brokenly. "You can't realize the need we have for this money. My husband and I have had a very hard time this winter."

George had gone to the limousine with Miss Dana. The girls were just bidding good-bye to the Reids, when there came a knock at the back door. Instantly, as if they were sensing the identity of their visitor, the farmer and his wife became tense. Mrs. Reid excused herself and a moment later called her husband to the door.

Louise and Jean could not see the man who had arrived but his gruff voice reached them plainly.

"I've listened to your excuses long enough," he was saying to the Reids. "You're five months behind in your rent for the farm. The figure amounts to three hundred and ninety dollars. Either you pay now or prepare to move out."

"We'll give you fifty dollars," the farmer said pleadingly. "It's every cent we can raise just now."

"Fifty dollars won't do. I'll give you six days to get your stuff packed."

Evangeline, angered by the attitude of the landlord, took a step as if to intercede for the Reids. Then, changing her mind, she turned to Louise and Jean.

"We can't let him dispossess this kind old couple," she whispered. "I am going to help them."

Taking four crisp new bills from her purse she thrust them into Louise's hand.

"Give these to Mrs. Reid," she urged. "Then hurry to the car before she has time to refuse the gift."

CHAPTER XXI

Lost

THE assignment was one very much to the liking of the Dana girls. Entering the kitchen they approached Mrs. Reid and slipped the money into the hand of the astonished woman.

"You have given me four hundred dollars!" she exclaimed.

"The gift is not from us," explained Louise. "It is from the friend who is with us."

"Who is this mysterious friend?" questioned the landlord shrewdly. "Some rich lady? I noticed a big car in the yard as I came up the lane."

Jean and Louise smiled but did not answer the question for they knew Miss Warrington did not wish to have her name revealed. Urging Mrs. Reid to keep the money, they listened to her outpouring of gratitude, then hastened to the car.

"Drive away quickly, George," commanded Miss Warrington, as soon as the Danas had seated themselves.

The chauffeur had obtained complete road information from Mr. Reid. In accordance with the instructions he turned the way the party had come the previous evening. An hour's ride brought the limousine to the fork in the highway which had puzzled them previously. From that point travel was much easier, but the detour was a long one. To complicate matters, it soon began to snow and the windshield wiper failed to work properly. The man was unable to fix it and several times he had to get out of the car and clean the glass with a cloth.

"We'll stop at the first garage we come to and have repairs made," Miss Warrington declared. "It shouldn't take long. Aren't these delays annoying?"

Before the auto had reached the end of the detour, snow was falling so fast that George had difficulty in seeing beyond the headlights which he had been forced to turn on. Miss Dana leaned forward tensely, straining her eyes in an attempt to watch the road.

"Now, Aunt Harriet, we have a good driver," Jean said soothingly. "Please don't worry. Nothing will happen."

"I can't help it. I've never seen a worse storm. Furthermore it would be sheer folly for you girls to start off afoot in this weather."

"It doesn't seem to be a sensible idea," agreed Jean reluctantly.

Ten minutes later the car struck pavement and entered a small town at the base of a mountain. Noticing a hotel on the main street, Miss Warrington ordered the chauffeur to stop there.

"There is no purpose in trying to go on in this blizzard," she declared in a resigned tone. "We may as well make ourselves comfortable while George has the windshield wiper repaired. As soon as the storm lets up we'll continue."

Tramping inside the building, Miss Dana and the girls warmed themselves by the open fire. Not wishing to engage rooms, they bought a supply of magazines, bars of chocolate and other articles that were on sale at a stand in the lobby.

"While we are here I'll telephone to Mr. Mc-Carter," Evangeline said, becoming restless during the wait. "If he doesn't receive word from us he may think we have run into trouble."

Fortunately the young woman succeeded in getting the call through. After talking with the detective for several minutes she was somewhat surprised at his request to speak to one of the Dana girls. Jean, who was standing near, took the phone and listened intently.

"I asked for you because I didn't want to worry Miss Warrington," Mr. McCarter explained hurriedly.

"Have you learned something alarming?" Jean inquired. She spoke in a low tone, as Evangeline was almost within earshot.

"Nothing about Mr. Warrington. But last night his private study was broken into at the Manor house," the man replied.

"What was taken?" the girl whispered.

"Nothing, so far as I can discover. I haven't completed my check-up yet. Several files of letters and papers were ransacked."

"How did the intruder enter?"

"That's the puzzling part. Bert Badger claims no one tried to get through the gate and I'm inclined to accept his story. Of course, he could have fallen asleep while on guard."

"Badger is a faithful servant."

"Yes, he seems to be," the detective acknowledged. "There's something mighty queer about the way things are going on, though."

After Jean reported the conversation to Louise the girls discussed the matter in private. They too were puzzled by the strange happenings.

For two hours the storm did not abate; rather it kept on unceasingly. Then, as Evangeline and her friends were about to abandon all hope of any change in the weather, the skies miraculously cleared and the sun broke through the clouds.

The windshield wiper had been repaired, so the car started on once more, the girls and Miss Dana breathing sighs of relief to be on their way. The mountain road wound in easy circles upward, hemmed in by tall, snow-caked evergreens. Every curve offered an inspiring view of rolling plains, white and attractive under the glistening blanket. When the travelers came to the end of the road, George parked the limou-

sine in a clump of cedars. He held the door
open for them.

"You are to wait here until we return," Miss
Warrington instructed the colored man. "We'll
try to get back in an hour. It may take us a
little longer."

Jean and Louise felt that their aunt would
be more comfortable in the car, but Miss Dana
insisted upon accompanying the girls on their
trek to the mysterious cabin.

"The mission is too dangerous a one for you
to attempt alone," she said firmly. "I haven't
done any mountain climbing in years but I
should be able to walk a mile or so."

Leaving George with the car, the party set off
through the deep snow. Upon reaching the first
ridge the girls paused to get their bearings.
Immediately opinion became divided. Louise
and Evangeline wished to go in one direction,
while Jean and her Aunt Harriet favored taking the opposite course.

After discussion a route was chosen, and the
group started through a pine woods. As they
came to a tiny clearing Louise saw a building
some distance ahead of them.

"We guessed correctly," she exclaimed in
triumph. "I think I see the cabin."

Cheered, the four pushed on but had not gone
far before they realized their error. The struc-
ture which Louise had seen was not a shack but
an abandoned sawmill.

"This can't be right," murmured Jean, pausing. "That map we had didn't indicate a sawmill, I'm sure."

"Apparently we're far off the trail," admitted Louise ruefully. "I hope we haven't followed the wrong mountain road."

"One thing is clear," said Miss Dana firmly. "We can't tramp aimlessly through the woods searching for a will-o'-the-wisp cabin. We might lose our way."

"I suppose it would be wise to return to the car," replied Louise reluctantly. "Oh, dear, this adventure hasn't turned out the way we planned. I'm so disappointed."

"And all because we lost the map," Jean added in discouragement. "If only Lettie hadn't torn it up. I'm sure she did it on purpose!"

As the girls retraced their way they noticed that Miss Dana was walking with increasing difficulty. Her nieces took turns helping her, but even so she was forced to pause frequently to get her breath and rest.

"I didn't think a little hike like this would upset me so," she gasped at last. "I am almost exhausted from it."

"We've come a long distance," returned Louise, glancing anxiously about her. "But the car should be somewhere close by."

The girls had not paid much attention to the high wind which was causing the snow to drift.

Their own footprints no longer were visible. Soon Jean dropped back from the head of the line to whisper to her sister.

"Louise, we're lost!"

"We can't be, Jean. The car isn't far away, I'm sure."

"I realize that, but Evangeline and I haven't any idea which way to go. Are *you* sure of the trail?"

"No, I'm not. I didn't pay much attention to it because I thought we could follow our own tracks back."

"It seems to me the wisest thing for us to do would be to shout," suggested Jean. "George may hear us."

"I hate to alarm Aunt Harriet."

"So do I, but we can't keep tramping around in circles. She is nearly exhausted."

Miss Dana accepted the news most philosophically.

"I've feared for the past ten minutes that we are lost," she told the girls. "We'll all shout together and perhaps the chauffeur will hear us."

The four raised their voices in unison but the only sound to come back was the howl of the wind. Actually, George had fallen asleep in the car beyond the next ridge and consequently did not hear a sound.

Several times the girls called out loudly.

Then, becoming discouraged, they tramped on
through the deep drifts.

"Why not break up into two parties?" suggested Jean desperately. "That way some of
us might reach the car and bring help."

"No, we had better stay together," Miss
Dana said firmly. "It would be foolhardy for
us to separate."

Wearily and doggedly the party trudged on,
pausing often to rest. The wind was cold and
penetrated even heavy clothing.

"Listen!" Louise suddenly commanded.

For a hopeful moment the others believed
Louise had heard the voice of a rescuer. Then
a sound reached their ears that caused them to
become sick at heart. It was the cry of a wild
animal. From the intensity of the scream they
knew that the beast was not very far away.

CHAPTER XXII

INSIDE THE SAFE

"RUN!" commanded Evangeline fearfully as the weird cry was heard again.

The four started to plunge through the snow, but before they had gone a dozen yards Miss Dana slipped on a patch of ice and twisted her ankle. Jean helped her aunt to her feet, but the woman gave a moan of anguish as she tried to walk.

"Go on without me," she murmured, sinking down in the snow. "I can't make it."

Of course her nieces would not desert their aunt. Knowing full well they could not hope to carry her very far through the deep drifts, they realized their situation was a precarious one indeed.

"Let's shout once more for help," proposed Jean desperately.

Again the girls raised their voices. This time they succeeded in arousing the sleeping chauffeur whose car was hidden by the tall evergreens. Immediately he tooted the horn several times.

"Thank goodness!" exclaimed Jean in relief.

"We were close to the automobile all the time and didn't realize it."

"I can walk that far if you'll help me," Miss Dana said courageously.

Supported by Louise and Jean she hobbled on. In a few minutes the party reached the car safely.

"We must take you to a doctor, Aunt Harriet," the older niece declared as she examined the twisted ankle.

"Oh, dear," Miss Dana sighed. "I've proven to be a great hindrance on this trip. I didn't expect things to turn out this way."

"Now don't blame yourself," Jean said instantly. "I feel certain our trip would have been in vain in any case. Obviously we've taken the wrong road."

"Mr. McCarter must have been mistaken," added Evangeline. "Usually he is so correct in anything he says."

The trip down the icy mountain road consumed three quarters of an hour. At the town of Cordell the girls found a doctor who bandaged Miss Dana's ankle. His diagnosis was not encouraging.

"I should advise several days in bed," he said firmly after he had finished. "Complications may arise if that is not done."

After some discussion it was decided by the girls that the only sensible thing to do would be to abandon the trip and drive Miss Dana to

her home at Oak Falls. By consulting a map
the girls learned that they could shorten the
distance a great many miles by taking a ferry.

Favored by good roads all the way, the party
made excellent time, arriving in Oak Falls at
dusk. After Miss Dana had been made comfortable and left in the care of Cora Appel and
a neighbor, the Penfield group started back.

Hours later Evangeline and the Dana girls
reached their destination. As the limousine
drew up at Warrington Manor, Bert Badger
swung wide the gate.

"Has anything of importance occurred here
while I've been gone?" Evangeline asked the
man eagerly.

"I guess you'll get a complete report from
Mr. McCarter," the lodge keeper answered
evasively.

From the way the man spoke Louise and Jean
gained the impression that he had significant
news to report, but was hesitant about alarming
his mistress. Accordingly at the first opportunity they slipped back to the gatehouse to talk
with him.

"There's something funny going on at this
place," he confided readily enough. "For one
thing, it was strange about Mr. Warrington's
den being entered. I have an idea, though
there may be nothing to it."

"What is your idea?" Jean asked curiously.
"Any clue will help."

"Well, I'll tell you a secret. This gatehouse has a hidden wall safe."

The sisters smiled, for the information did not surprise them. They waited for Bert Badger to tell them more.

"I have a hunch that if a fellow could get into the safe he might find something that would help Mr. Warrington's case."

Louise and Jean nodded in agreement as the gatekeeper resumed:

"The past two days I've heard a prowler around this place. It looks to me as if he's after something. But whatever you do don't tell Miss Warrington. I wouldn't want to add to her worries."

"Can you describe the person?" Louise questioned hopefully.

The gateman shook his head. "No, I didn't get a good look at the fellow. As soon as he saw me he ran. But I'm satisfied someone is here looking for evidence in the safe. I've been trying to open it myself."

"Any luck?" asked Jean quickly.

"Not yet."

"I wish we had the combination," Jean murmured thoughtfully. "Mr. Warrington doubtless has it. Perhaps that is why his den was entered. Someone was searching for it."

The Dana girls shared Badger's belief that the wall safe might hold a key to the mystery. They had not forgotten the note sent by Mr.

Warrington to Mrs. Zerbe in which he had referred to a "secret at the gatehouse."

Upon returning to the main house, Louise and Jean had a long talk with Evangeline. Without revealing their purpose or any of the information given them by Badger, they obtained permission from the young woman to search through Mr. Warrington's private study. For two hours the girls examined papers and documents in systematic fashion.

"I can't figure out what you expect to find," Evangeline remarked in a baffled tone.

"I guess we don't know ourselves," Louise responded lightly. "At any rate we haven't found a thing yet that is any clue."

At that moment Jean, in looking through the contents of the last unexamined drawer of Mr. Warrington's desk, came upon a tiny red leather notebook containing various notations. Without attracting Evangeline's attention she slipped it into her pocket.

Later that night when they were in the room assigned to them, the Dana girls examined the little book from cover to cover. They were highly elated to discover upon one of the pages a series of numbers.

"That looks to me as if it might be the combination of a safe!" Jean cried in delight.

"It does! I wish we could try it out!"

"Well, why don't we?" proposed Jean boldly.

"We'll never have a better opportunity than now."

"That's so. Tomorrow we'll be back at Starhurst again," agreed her sister.

Jean moved toward the door. "I'll ask Evangeline to go down there with us."

Louise grasped the younger girl's hand, pulling her back.

"No. Don't you think it would be much wiser to go there by ourselves? Suppose we should discover evidence detrimental to Mr. Warrington's case?"

"I hadn't considered that angle."

"Evangeline would not thank us for interfering. Any such information would come to her as a great shock."

"You're right," Jean agreed. "We ought to play a lone hand in this game. The question is, will Bert Badger cooperate with us?"

"He should. He's as eager as we are to help the Warringtons."

"I realize that," admitted Jean, frowning. "But he doesn't know much about us. He may decide that we're trying to further our own ends."

"Between us we should be able to convince him. However, we must be careful that Evangeline or the servants do not see us going down to the gatehouse," warned Louise.

The girls turned out their bedroom light and

sat by the window waiting for the members of the household to retire. Shortly before midnight the last light in the place was extinguished.

After hesitating a little longer, the sisters stole noiselessly down the main stairway. The front door was locked but they were able to unsnap the catch and steal outside. It was biting cold, though clear.

"The gatehouse is dark," Jean whispered as the sisters huddled together on the porch. "Badger must have gone to bed."

"Then we'll wake him up."

Moving stealthily across the lawn, the girls glanced about carefully to be certain they were not being observed. To all appearances the grounds were deserted, yet they could not rid themselves of a feeling that they were being watched.

"The lodge keeper's talk of prowlers has made us nervous," Jean said with a giggle. "That shows what the power of suggestion will do."

"Yet someone must have been snooping about this place," Louise replied soberly. "The mystery to me is how the fellow gets in and out of the place without being caught."

"He may have a key. It seems fairly clear, too, that whoever the person is he's after important evidence hidden in the gatehouse. I only hope we'll be able to get the safe open."

The girls had drawn close to the stone building. Louise lowered her voice as she answered:

"Jean, if we do succeed in opening the safe
let's keep our information from Badger. While
he is loyal, it's just as well he doesn't know too
much about the Warringtons' private affairs."

Since the windows of the gatehouse were dark,
the girls went to the side door and rapped
loudly.

"Who is there?" called a man's voice.

Louise and Jean gave their names, but apparently the keeper did not understand, for the next
instant Badger flung open the door and faced
the girls with a drawn revolver.

"Hands up!" he commanded grimly. "And
be quick, or I'll fire!"

CHAPTER XXIII

The Secret at the Gatehouse

For one instant the sisters were startled.

"Don't you know us?" cried Jean without obeying the order. "We're friends—Louise and Jean Dana."

"I can't see you out there in the dark," the gatekeeper muttered. "Raise your hands and step into the light."

This time the two girls obeyed. As the man obtained a clear view of their faces he put aside his revolver and apologized.

"I hope I didn't frighten you," he said. "I thought you were prowlers trying to break into the place again."

"You frightened us for a moment," Louise admitted ruefully.

"What brings you here at this time of night?" Badger inquired abruptly. "Did Miss Warrington send you?"

Jean shook her head. "No, it is our own idea. We think we may be able to open the safe," she said.

"It's not likely. I've tried half a dozen times without any luck."

"We're not sure, but we believe we have the combination," declared Louise. "Since we

192

shouldn't be interrupted while we are trying to open it, I wonder if you would stand guard outside the building to make certain no one watches us from the window.''

"Sure," the man broke in quickly, "that's the only reliable way. I'll keep a close lookout."

Never suspecting that the girls wished to be rid of him, Bert Badger pulled on a heavy coat and stepped out into the cold. Highly elated, Louise and Jean worked swiftly. They brought a screen from an adjoining room and placed it so that it would shield their actions from the gatekeeper should he peer through the window.

Only an instant was required for Jean to lift down the heavy picture from the wall. Then she opened the panel. While her sister read off the numbers to her, she began to fumble with the dial of the safe.

"You'll have to do it, Louise," the younger girl declared at last. "I'm so excited I can't keep my hand steady. I've made a mistake."

They shifted places and Jean called out the numbers of the combination. As Louise twisted the dial for the final time they heard a sharp little click.

"There, it's unlocked!" she whispered jubilantly.

"Sh!" warned her sister.

The safe door swung open. At first glance both girls were bitterly disappointed for the interior appeared to be empty. As Louise groped about, her hand encountered a large book which she brought to light.

"A Bible!" exclaimed Jean in astonishment. "Perhaps it contains family records."

Eagerly the girls scanned the first pages of the huge leather-bound volume. Almost at once they came upon a notation written in faded ink. Both girls stared at it.

"Jean, we've found the key to the mystery at last!" Louise whispered in awe as they re-read the words recorded in the Bible.

"We've learned the secret of the gatehouse," added Jean, fairly beside herself with excitement. "What will Evangeline say when she hears the truth?" she asked.

"For the time being she mustn't know. It would be unwise for us to tell anyone until the proper moment arrives."

"You're right," nodded Jean. "But when we do drop our bombshell——"

The outside door of the gatehouse opened and Bert Badger peered inside.

"How you making out?" he called in a low tone.

"We've opened the safe," Louise replied, thrusting the Bible back into its former place. "There's no treasure."

Hurriedly she closed the door and twisted the dial. The gatekeeper came into the room.

"Empty, eh?" he asked. "I was afraid it would turn out that way, but I'm just as glad.

I shouldn't like to be responsible for anything valuable being kept in this place—not with prowlers trying to break in all the time. I won't be so worried after this."

"It might be well to keep a close watch of the building even so," suggested Louise soberly. "An intruder may be after something else."

"Oh, I'll do that," the man declared. "I'm not one to neglect my duties."

"Don't tell anyone we were here this evening," Jean warned as she and her sister prepared to leave.

"Later on we'll tell Miss Warrington ourselves," added Louise.

"I'll keep it mum," Badger promised.

Without attracting attention to themselves, the girls returned to the main house and slipped into their room. Tumbling into bed they slept soundly for the remainder of the night and did not awaken until they heard voices in the adjoining room occupied by Miss Warrington.

"I'm sorry to disturb you so early, Miss Evangeline," the housekeeper was saying. "But I am afraid someone entered the house again."

"What makes you think so?" questioned the young woman. "Is anything missing?"

"Not that I can discover. However, the front hall is tracked with mud, and I distinctly remember brushing off the carpet just before I went to bed last night."

"I'll get right up and investigate," promised Miss Warrington.

Later, when Jean and Louise went downstairs to breakfast, they heard the servants discussing the mysterious intruder. Evangeline reported the incident to the Danas. The girls offered non-committal responses and kept their secret to themselves.

Shortly after nine o'clock Mr. McCarter arrived at the mansion. Keen was his disappointment upon learning that the girls had failed to reach the mountain cabin.

"To tell you the truth," he said gravely, "the committee investigating Mr. Warrington's business affairs has begun to lose patience. They've given me to understand that unless we produce Mr. Warrington within forty-eight hours the entire matter will be made public through the newspapers."

"They believe we know his whereabouts and won't reveal them?" asked Evangeline, aghast.

"Yes, I've tried to make them listen to reason but without much success. Unless your father's hiding place is revealed within the next two days a sensational story will be published by the press."

Miss Warrington broke down and cried freely. "Then we must do something!"

"We might try once more to locate the mountain lodge," declared Louise.

"The sooner we start the better," stated Mr.

McCarter briskly. "I'll go with you this time and we'll find it!"

"If only we could trace that hunter whose name we think is Thomas Farley he could lead us directly to the cabin," remarked Louise thoughtfully.

"We'll locate him," declared the detective confidently. "It won't be difficult."

Louise and Jean disliked missing another day of school, but they sensed that the Warrington case might be drawing to a conclusion. With the knowledge obtained from the gatehouse safe they felt an added sense of responsibility. Accordingly, when the detective urged them to accompany the party they readily agreed to do so.

Once more the limousine was ordered out. With the weather less cold and the roads clear of ice for long stretches, George made much faster time than upon the previous day. At Calumet Detective McCarter took charge of the search for Thomas Farley, finally locating him at a barber shop. He was indeed the hunter to whom the girls had spoken.

"Why certainly, I'll be glad to direct you to the cabin," the man said heartily when the request was made. "I can't understand why you were unable to locate the place yesterday. It's not hard to find."

With Mr. Farley accompanying them, the car raced to the foot of Kaleman's Mountain.

There George started to take the same road which had been followed the previous day.

"Hold on there," called Farley from the rear. "Now I see where you made your mistake. This road takes you to the opposite side of the mountain. Turn down the other highway."

For an hour the car climbed the steep, twisting road which finally ended.

"This is as far as we can ride," the hunter announced, opening the door. "We'll have to walk to the cabin from here."

"Is it much of a climb?" inquired Miss Warrington uneasily.

"Yes, it's a good hard hike and with the snow melting the trail may prove to be slippery."

Leaving George to look after the car, the party set off with Thomas Farley walking ahead to break the way. The drifts were deep in unprotected places and the snow was very damp. Now and then as they would pass near some rocky ledges, layers of them would loosen and drop down upon their heads.

"It's melting fast," the hunter remarked, glancing anxiously toward the summit of the mountain. "We must use more than ordinary caution not to get into trouble."

"Is there much danger?" Evangeline inquired nervously.

"Not if you watch your footing and the snow doesn't start to slide."

As the party climbed higher, the sun shone

brightly on them. Suddenly Thomas Farley, who was still in the lead, halted, and gave a shout of alarm.

"An avalanche! We'll be crushed beneath its weight!"

Following the man's horrified gaze, the others saw a mighty sheet of snow sliding down the mountainside directly above them!

CHAPTER XXIV

Prisoners

"Quick! Get under the ledge!" shouted the hunter. "Huddle close to the wall."

As the five climbers flattened themselves against the rock, a great white mass thundered down the mountainside, directly over the place where they had stood a moment before. For a long while it poured over the ledge like a huge waterfall, then subsided. Cautiously the hunter came from the shelter.

"It's safe now," he told the others in relief. "We certainly had a close call."

"How much farther is it to the cabin?" Miss Warrington questioned shakily.

"Not more than a quarter of a mile. I doubt that we'll encounter any sliding snow again."

Evangeline and the Dana girls walked with the greatest caution, as did the hunter. However, Detective McCarter was more reckless. Before they had gone very far he slipped on a piece of ice, which caused him to slide toward a deep crevasse. Fortunately he acted instinctively to save himself, by catching hold of a rocky projection above the yawning hole. He clung there until Farley and the Dana girls were able to pull him out of danger.

The incident served to unnerve every member of the group. It was a great relief to them when a bend in the trail revealed the first glimpse of the mysterious cabin.

"No smoke is coming from the chimney," observed Jean as they paused to consider their next move. "The place looks deserted."

"That's funny," remarked Thomas Farley. "It was occupied only a few days ago. You can see footprints in the snow even now."

"They seem to be leading away from the cabin," pointed out Louise before McCarter could voice a similar observation.

"The man who lives there may have gone after game or supplies. If he is absent this ought to be a good time to investigate the place," suggested the detective.

Thomas Farley started forward, only to have the other man place a restraining hand on his shoulder.

"Wait a minute. It isn't wise for us all to go. We might walk into a trap," McCarter advised.

"Why not let Louise and me go to the door first?" demanded Jean eagerly. "If anyone answers we'll say we are school girls out hiking and we'd like a drink of water. Our story ought not to arouse anyone's suspicion."

"You're not afraid to try it?" the detective asked admiringly.

"Not a bit."

Louise eagerly agreed to her sister's plan.

"Then the rest of us will stay here and keep watch," declared Detective McCarter. "If you need help, one of you wave or raise your right hand as a signal."

Excitedly the Dana girls struggled through the deep snow toward the cabin. They listened for a moment at the door but could hear no sound from within. Then Jean rapped several times.

"No one seems to be here," she stated after they had waited a few minutes.

"Let's try to get inside," suggested Louise.

Jean twisted the door handle and pushed her weight against the panel.

"It's locked," she whispered.

"We could break a pane and open a window," Louise said, walking to one on the opposite side of the shack. "The whole mystery is important enough for us to get inside and find out whether or not Mr. Warrington has been here, if we can."

She smashed one small pane with a piece of wood she found near at hand. Reaching her hand inside, she managed to unfasten and raise the window.

"The place surely is deserted," she observed, thrusting her head through the opening. "Otherwise this noise would have brought someone here."

Jean raised Louise up and in turn was helped through the window. The girls found themselves in a cold, barren cabin sparsely and bleakly furnished with only a crudely made table, a couple of chairs and a cot. The fire was out although the ashes still smoldered on the hearth. Dishes evidently used that day had not been washed.

A ladder led to a loft. Jean climbed up and soon returned to report that place also deserted.

"Whoever was here can't have been gone many hours—" Louise began, only to break off as she and her sister heard a strange sound coming from beneath the floor.

"What was that?" whispered Jean, drawing closer to Louise.

As they waited tensely the girls distinctly heard the noise again. This time they were certain someone was moaning as if in pain.

"The cabin must have a cellar," Louise whispered excitedly.

Noticing a door which had not been investigated she tiptoed to it. Turning a key in the lock, she swung it open softly.

"Help! Help!" called a muffled voice, barely audible.

"Mr. Warrington may be held a prisoner down there!" Jean said excitedly. "Whoever he is, we must get him out!"

In her haste she started down the dark stairway without noticing that one of the steps was almost worn away. Missing her footing, she stumbled and could not save herself. Head

over heels she tumbled to the very bottom, landing on the floor of the cellar.

"Jean, are you hurt?" Louise gasped.
Quickly she grabbed a flashlight from her purse
and hurried below to help her sister.

"Not badly," Jean muttered, picking herself
up. "I skinned my elbow a little."

"Listen!" commanded Louise, standing mo-
tionless.

In the far end of the cellar they could hear
someone moving. Then there came a low moan
of anguish.

"Who is there?" Louise called sharply.

"Warrington. Help me!"

"Mr. Warrington!" cried the Danas in unison.

Reassured, the girls groped their way through
the dark until they came upon a man who had
been shackled with steel handcuffs. He was fas-
tened securely to a post which supported the
floor above.

"We can't get you out," Louise said after a
moment of effort. "Detective McCarter is outside. He will have to remove these cuffs first."

"I'll go back and signal to the others," Jean
offered.

Darting up the stairway, she ran to the window and waved her hand. Waiting only long
enough to make sure that Evangeline and the
two men understood her gesture, she hurried to
the cellar.

"How is Mr. Warrington?" she asked Louise in an undertone.

"He seems to be in a half dazed condition. Since you left he has not spoken a word nor even groaned."

"Probably he has been almost starved," Jean said angrily. "Who do you suppose could have done this to him?"

"My guess would be Nat Kaner."

The girls spoke encouraging words to Mr. Warrington until the others arrived. Evangeline was very happy to find her father, but heartbroken at his pitiful plight. Observing his wretched condition, she could not control her tears.

"Father! Don't you know me?" she pleaded, kneeling beside him. "It's Eve. Speak, Father."

"Eve," he murmured, feebly taking his daughter's hand. He could say no more.

"We'll soon get you out of here," declared Mr. McCarter.

Having no key with him to unlock the steel cuffs the detective set to work filing them apart.

"Did you hear a sound overhead?" Jean presently inquired.

Louise listened for a moment, then said, "You must have imagined it. I heard nothing."

Jean really had discerned footsteps on the cabin floor above them. Unknown to those in the cellar, Nat Kaner had returned to the shack soon after the rescue party had disappeared from view.

Approaching with the utmost caution he noticed the broken window pane and instantly divined that aid had come for Mr. Warrington. The first thought of the former valet was to make his escape.

As he peered through the open window he observed that the main floor of the cabin was deserted. Moving stealthily inside he tiptoed to the cellar door and listened intently. Satisfied as to the identity of the persons who were in the basement he chuckled wickedly.

"I'll teach them not to try to get the best of Nat Kaner!" he hissed.

Softly the man eased the door shut and turned the key in the lock. Then, fearful that the panels might be rammed when the prisoners should learn of their plight, he further barricaded the exit with a heavy table.

"There, that ought to hold them!" he muttered, taking a match from his pocket. "I wish I could stay and watch, but I'll not risk it. By the time the fire is discovered I must be a long way from here!"

CHAPTER XXV

A Vital Revelation

Nat Kaner kindled a fire near the cellar doorway. Waiting only long enough to be certain that the flames would spread, he stole away from the cabin.

Meanwhile, the rescue party had succeeded at last in freeing Mr. Warrington. As Detective McCarter and Thomas Farley raised the man to his feet he began to mutter in a strange, half delirious manner. He did not seem to notice those about him, but stared into space.

"—Not who you think I am—all these years—punished for something which wasn't my fault. Not a true Warrington—ought to tell——"

"Poor Father," Evangeline murmured brokenly, "his sufferings have affected him. He doesn't know what he is saying."

In the darkness Jean squeezed her sister's hand in understanding. While they offered no comment, the girls knew that Mr. Warrington was not out of his mind. The time would come soon when the secret they had learned at the gatehouse would have to be told.

While Evangeline and the two men aided the

victim of the kidnaper, the Danas hastened up the stairway. Finding the door closed, Jean tried to open it. To her horror it was locked.

Suddenly the girls were alarmed at the odor of burning wood. Simultaneously they noticed smoke creeping beneath the wide crack at the bottom of the door.

"We've been locked into the cellar!" Louise shouted. "And the cabin is on fire!"

Abandoning Mr. Warrington to Evangeline's care, the two men leaped up the stairway. Detective McCarter tested the strength of the door and hurled his powerful frame against it.

"See if you can find a ram," he said hoarsely to Thomas Farley. "If we don't get out of here quickly we'll be burned to death!"

Louise and Jean aided in the frantic search but the cellar was bare. They found nothing they could use to shove through the panels of the door. Working together, the two men tried desperately to break it down but their efforts were unavailing.

In a very few minutes the air was heavy with smoke. The crackling sound of flames had risen to a roar.

"We're finished," Detective McCarter said, sinking exhausted on the steps. "There's no possible way for us to get out."

For the space of several minutes no one spoke. Then from above the roar of the fire Louise thought she heard a voice. The cry seemed to come from overhead. Her heart beat high with hope. As she listened tensely the call came a second time.

"Hello! Anyone here?"

In an instant all the trapped group were on their feet, shouting and clamoring for help. It seemed an eternity before the cellar door was flung open, revealing a wall of flame. A man staggered through the smoke.

"Quick!" he shouted, grasping Jean by the arm. "This cabin is an inferno!"

With the men carrying Mr. Warrington, a dash was made through the flames. Reaching safety, the Dana girls saw that their rescuers were three forest rangers.

"We noticed the blaze from our lookout tower," one of them said.

Before anyone could express his gratitude for this miraculous deliverance from death, Mr. Warrington, his strength overtaxed, slumped into a faint. It was several minutes before he could be revived. By that time it was too late to save anything from the cabin. One after the other the flaming walls collapsed.

"We must get Father into the car at once," said Evangeline anxiously. "He needs the care of a doctor."

"Who imprisoned you, Mr. Warrington?" questioned the detective.

With an effort the victim answered, "My former valet, Nat Kaner."

"It must have been he who locked us in the cellar," Mr. McCarter said grimly. "He can't be far away from here."

Learning the details of what had occurred, the three rangers volunteered to trail Kaner and bring him to justice. Their offer was gratefully accepted by the detective, who felt unable to cope with the unfamiliar mountain conditions.

Mr. Warrington was assisted to the waiting limousine and taken with all possible speed to his estate. There he was put to bed and a doctor summoned. While the man had suffered severely from his long confinement, everyone was relieved to learn that rest and good food soon would restore the man's strength.

Late in the afternoon Evangeline told Louise and Jean that her father wished to speak with them alone. Accordingly they went to the bedroom where the man sat propped up with pillows. He motioned for them to seat themselves beside him.

"First of all, I want to thank you for having saved my life," he began, speaking with difficulty. "And I should like to ask a favor of you."

"We'll do anything we can to help you," declared Louise heartily.

"My affairs are in a turbulent state, due to the underhanded work of Nat Kaner and his brother Mortimer. I foolishly trusted my valet who also acted as a secretary, and until very

recently did not suspect that he had been sign-
ing my name to various checks and documents
without my consent. That, however, is beside
the point. I called you here to talk about Eve.
There is something I must tell her and I fear it
will prove a great shock to the poor child.''

"I think we understand," murmured Jean.

"You couldn't possibly know that my true
name is not Warrington?" the man asked in a
shocked tone.

"We learned it last night," revealed Louise
quietly. "But you need have no fear we will
disclose your secret to anyone."

"How did you find out?"

"From the Bible kept in hiding at the gatehouse."

"I see," nodded Mr. Warrington. "Then I
hardly need explain."

"There are many details which we fail to
understand," Jean replied. "Perhaps you
wouldn't mind telling us the entire story."

"You have a right to know. Please believe me
when I say that I had no intention of deceiving
people. I did not learn the truth myself until
Mrs. Zerbe told me everything a short time before her death. As you discovered in the records of the family Bible, I am the son of Mrs.
Zerbe and her husband.

"According to the Warrington tradition, a
son always has inherited the Manor house and
the fortune. My parents—that is," he corrected

himself, "the Warringtons had no child of their own for a long time after their marriage and were in despair lest they never have an heir. After many years a son was born to them, but the baby was puny and died within a few hours after birth."

"Was Doctor Morgan the attending physician?" interposed Louise as the speaker paused in his narrative.

"Yes, the kindly old doctor realized that the shock of learning her baby was dead might kill Mrs. Warrington. It so happened that Mrs. Zerbe gave birth to a son almost the same day and Doctor Morgan looked after her too. Knowing that Mrs. Zerbe was morose because she believed her child never would have a chance in the world without money, he proposed a substitution of infants."

"And did Mrs. Zerbe agree to the plan?" questioned Jean in surprise.

"Not at first, but when she learned that Mrs. Warrington might die unless the idea were carried through she consented. It gave her great satisfaction to know that her son would become the master of Warrington Manor. I only wish I had learned the truth many, many years ago."

"At least you have peace of mind in knowing that you were kind to her always," returned Louise sympathetically.

"Shortly before she left Penfield Mrs. Zerbe told me the truth," Mr. Warrington went on with his story. "She said that only Doctor Morgan and herself knew of the substitution and that I must never tell anyone. Now I am aware that my valet, Nat Kaner, overheard at least a part of the conversation."

"Then he tried to blackmail you?" asked Jean eagerly.

"I imagine that was his intention. He began to annoy Mrs. Zerbe, trying to force her to reveal information."

"After the poor woman's death he tried to steal her luggage," added Louise.

"He gained nothing by that trick," said Mr. Warrington. "She never carried revealing papers."

"I suppose he is the person who has been trying to get into the gatehouse," nodded Jean thoughtfully. "He suspected that the evidence was hidden there."

"You see the position I am in now," continued Mr. Warrington sadly. "I can go before the inquiry board and tell the truth about Nat Kaner and our relationship. I'll be able to clear myself but at a cost. Eve must learn the truth. I cannot rightfully claim the Warrington name nor fortune any longer."

Before either Jean or Louise could offer sympathy, the bedroom door was flung open. Evangeline ran to her father and fell to her knees at his bedside.

"Forgive me for listening," she murmured.

"I heard everything you said, Father. It doesn't matter to me *who* you are. I am proud and happy that you are honest, and are able to prove it before the world!"

Louise and Jean waited to hear no more. They felt that such an intimate scene as this should have no witnesses. Quietly they stole from the room and went downstairs where they found Detective McCarter waiting to talk with them.

"I have good news," he reported gaily. "Nat Kaner has been caught and has made a complete confession. He and his brother are certain to be sent to prison. The trial will be a mere formality."

"Will Mr. Warrington's name be cleared?" Jean asked in relief.

"Yes, Kaner's confession cleans up the case. He has taken all the blame for causing the tangle in Mr. Warrington's business affairs. The investigation will be dropped."

"That *is* wonderful news," laughed Jean.

"The case most certainly would not have ended so satisfactorily if you two young ladies hadn't taken a hand. I'm proud to have been associated with you," said Mr. McCarter, shaking hands with each of the girls and remarking in a half serious way that if ever he needed help again he would call upon them.

Before returning to Starhurst, the Dana girls assigned themselves a special task. They slipped down to the gatehouse while Bert Badger was in another part of the grounds. Deftly they opened the safe and from the Bible removed all the records revealing Mr. Warrington's true parentage.

"There," said Jean as she dropped the pages into the fireplace and watched them burn, "no one ever need know. Mr. Warrington's secret will be safe forever."

"The secret at the gatehouse has become the secret of the fireplace," added Louise dramatically.

"But not a secret fireplace," laughed Jean. "Wouldn't that be a wonderful place for a mystery?"

Her sister agreed lightly, not knowing that in the near future the girls would become involved in a case to be given the very name of The Mysterious Fireplace.

A noise from outside the gatehouse warned the girls to hurry. Hastily Louise replaced the Bible in the safe and closed the door. They ran outside expecting to meet Badger, but instead they saw a Great Dane streaking across the lawn.

"Why, it's Sally, I do believe!" exclaimed Jean in astonishment. "The gate is open a crack and she squeezed through."

"This will be a wonderful surprise for her mistress!"

"I call it a wonderful day for everyone,"

added Jean. "Mr. Warrington is home again, Nat Kaner has been captured, and we've had a marvelous adventure."

"There's one drawback."

"What is that, Louise?"

"We've missed several days of school, and now we'll have to study hard to make up for lost time."

Jean linked arms with her sister as they walked toward the Manor house to tell Mr. Warrington what they had just done.

"Oh, I don't mind," she said. "After all we've been through, a quiet life will seem rather nice."

"Until we start on our next mystery," laughed Louise.